"As Jean describes Hungry Heart's search to find her place in the Master's Kingdom, I often found myself stopping to reflect on my own travels as I read through this spiritual parable. For those seeking discernment, this book will help to raise important questions."

—The Reverend C.F. Meinschein
Lutheran Pastor

"A colorful, profound depiction of the sacred journey of a hungry heart for God…one of the most sensitive allegorical accounts of a Christian's pilgrimage since *Hind's Feet on High Places*. A tremendous read!"

—B. Love
WBYN-ALIVE Radio

"I was captivated by Mrs. Koberlein's previous books, but the intensity and beauty of this book steps beyond her previous works. *The Paradigm Quest* is thought-provoking and insightful, a quest for the new millennium."

—Dr. M.R. Sadigh
Psychologist, Author, *The Secret Path*

"Intriguing…unlike any book I've ever read. The main character moves from excitement to suspense, tension to uncertainty, loneliness, frustration, and so many of the situations we find ourselves in."

—J. Moser

"Engaging, challenging, delightful, yet deep…a quest worth taking."

—J.D. Miller
Evangelist

"Once I started to read it, I couldn't put it down. *The Paradigm Quest* is thought-provoking, yet entertaining. It allows one's imagination to interact with the journey and feel what it is like to search for meaning in one's life. I heartily recommend it."

—The Reverend K.N. Creasy
United Church of Christ Pastor

"This allegory reflects our own Christian struggle to find out what God's plan for us is and how we should serve Him. The book is delightful."

—J. Griffin

THE
PARADIGM
QUEST

Jean Koberlein

ISBN 1-58169-052-5
For Worldwide Distribution
Printed in the U.S.A.

Evergreen Press
An Imprint of Genesis Communications, Inc.
P.O. Box 91011 • Mobile, AL 36691
800-367-8203
E-mail: EvergreenBooks@aol.com
www.iEvergreenPress.com

TABLE OF CONTENTS

FOREWORD

No matter how electronically adept or media-oriented our society becomes in the years ahead, I believe that the art of storytelling will never die out. Our human imagination will always be captured by the simplicity of truth presented in a picture of words. There is something about showing life through allegories and stories that grabs our hearts and minds better than a dry recitation can. We, as humans, tend to relate through emotions and empathy to others' experiences. It is a level of learning on which every individual is equal. Jesus knew this; He Himself used parables to teach spiritual principles to the masses—with much success.

The great Christian allegories that have stood the test of time, including *A Pilgrim's Progress* and *Hinds' Feet on High Places,* all have this anointed ability to slip lessons on Christian spirituality into the deepest corners of our hearts through their stories. Although it would be premature to class this newest allegory with such historical greats, *The Paradigm Quest* also holds this ability to drop truth into our hearts. Each time I read through this story, I found it more and more compelling. The experiences of Hungry Heart, an ordinary citizen in the kingdom of Christianity, related to mine. Her journey for understanding of her paradigm, in a sense, became my journey. What truth will come next in her search for her paradigm? What lesson will I learn next? What is my paradigm and life assignment? For both of us, nothing less than understanding of the Master's own heart will satisfy.

If you are a hungry heart—if you want to know more, learn more, understand more—then no matter where you are in your own walk with Jesus Christ, you will find your place in this story. *The Paradigm Quest* will encourage you to press on to the next level without fear. It will explain future paths you may have to take. And it will confirm to you that nothing less than the Master's own plan for your life will satisfy.

Finally, lest you have any misgivings about a writing such as this, let me assure you that I have known and worked with Jean Koberlein for a number of years. You can trust the principles she portrays in this book. They are researched from the Scriptures and have been lived out in her own life. In fact, I pray that we all may follow our own quests with as much grace as she has.

Jean, thank you for hearing and following the Master's plan in writing this book.

Jeanette M. Sprecher
Writer, Editor

INTRODUCTION

Just like the scientific law of gravity, the natural phenomena of cause and effect, and the spiritual principle of sowing and reaping, a paradigm is a philosophical or theoretical framework of reference. Newscasters and advertisers report "paradigm shifts" throughout the world on national, economic, and social levels. A paradigm is an "example or pattern."[1] Normally paradigms are intangible. We cannot see or touch them. They are described in terms of man's ideas and plans.

However, the paradigms in this story are not nearly as complicated as world affairs. These fictional paradigms are tangible. They are like emblematic jewelry, wedding rings, or religious symbols. For example, imagine yourself holding the scattered pieces of an unassembled yet exquisite jeweled watch. Some fragments are so small you can barely see them, yet each one is necessary. Perhaps a few are still missing. Over the years, a master watchmaker has given you each piece freely, one at a time, as he taught you about the piece's significance. One day a priceless watch will be assembled using those pieces, and the watchmaker will send you out to exhibit this beautiful watch all over the world. So your heart and mind are set in one direction: to obtain the missing pieces and fulfill your destiny, regardless of the cost.

This allegory is based on the biblical pattern (or spiritual paradigm) that Moses received from God on Mount Sinai in 1445 B.C.[2] One afternoon I listened to a Bible teacher explain that unless one studied the Tabernacle of Moses, the priestly garments, and the Feasts of Israel, it was impossible to fully understand the New Testament as it should be understood.

For the next two years I studied and taught these fascinating topics myself in small group studies. They radically changed my understanding of God's Word in many areas and helped me to put many of the scattered pieces of my own spiritual life in perspective. However, the myriad of details and facts continued to grow more complicated, and my files became thicker and thicker.

Although I felt God's call to write the account from an experiential perspective, as it speaks to our lives today, the wealth of information overwhelmed me. It did not happen overnight, but after several months of prayer, the Holy Spirit showed me how to glean prophetic truth from the historic passages of the Old Testament by following a young woman named Hungry Heart over three mountains. These mountains represent the three courts of the Tabernacle of Moses and form the foundation for this allegory.

Hungry Heart, the main character, is a typical citizen who has grown up securely in the kingdom of Christianity. Like almost every other individual in Christianity, she keeps a collection of paradigm pieces in a small blue pouch hanging over her heart. Hungry Heart received it years ago in a ceremony with the traditional words of remembrance: "Always keep the Master's truth close to your heart, when you rise up and when you lie down, when you walk by the way and when you stand in the midst. Never depart from it or allow it to depart from you."[3]

Every so often Hungry Heart pours out the contents of her little blue bag and tries to fit the pieces together. She, like many other hearts in this fictional kingdom, longs to complete her paradigm quest and find her place of appointment in the Master's service.

This is her story.

---

[1] "Example, pattern: esp: an outstandingly clear or typical example or archetype 2: an example of a conjugation or declension showing a word in all its inflectional forms 3: a philosophical and theoretical framework of a scientific school or discipline within which theories, laws, and generalizations and the experiments performed in support of them are formulated" (Merriam Webster's Collegiate Dictionary, 10th ed. [Springfield, Massachusetts: Merriam-Webster, Inc., 1996], 842).

[2] The Tabernacle of Moses (Ex. 25:8-9); the heavenly pattern (Heb. 8–9); and the revelation of Christ (Rev. 1:9-18).

[3] This application is based on Deuteronomy 11:18-20, Psalm 1 and many other Bible references that admonish the Christian to stay close to God's Word. Similar Christian precepts are woven throughout the text, however they are not biblical quotations.

DEDICATION

This book is lovingly dedicated to the small fellowship who gathered in our home in a quest to submit to the Refiner's fire. Jesus, the Son, was our one desire. Our journeys have all been unique over the past few years, and they have carried us from mountain to mountain, but our lives have never been the same. We have been through the fire. *The Paradigm Quest* is one small miracle these flames have produced to the glory of God.

PART ONE

THE
Quest Begins

CHAPTER 1

Facing the North Wind

Dark clouds pressed in from the north and threw deep shadows across the distant mountains like slithering tentacles of death. Normally the mountain peaks prevented such clouds from crossing the border countries and entering the kingdom of Christianity. Today, however, the sturdy evergreen trees on the slopes were literally forced to bow by the powerful winds that drove the stormy mass past the high peaks, down through the mountain crevices, and onto the plains, swallowing up every ray of afternoon sunshine in Hungry Heart's path.

"Look at the pitiful little fool. I'll bet you tomorrow's troubles that I can make her run. I can even make her run backwards if I want to."

"No, you can't—you're nothing but a wisp of hot air. Look at you! You can hardly cast a shadow, you stupid imp."

The two spirit creatures argued back and forth behind her, but Hungry Heart failed to realize how close the shadows had come.

"I tell you she's ready...we've got to attack while she's weak and scared. I'm gonna blow her paradigm pieces all over the valley! She'll be so scared, she won't know which one to try to save first. What fun—can't you just see her?"

"You're gonna shut up and be quiet—the North Wind is coming. When it does, it'll be a piece of cake for us to invade her heart." With that final word, the two dark creatures slipped back into the shadows and continued to follow Hungry Heart back to Grandfather's house.

Hungry Heart resisted the sudden urge to run. Nevertheless, she clutched her arms tightly together around her paradigm pouch to still her

2

shivering body as she tried to ignore the growing shadows quickly overtaking her in the strong wind. They were much darker than she had ever seen before. Fragments of stories about the foul spirits that lived in the Land of the Lost filtered into her mind. Hungry Heart had never actually seen a spirit creature, but she had heard the refugees from the border countries tell about the shapeless masses of evil that could easily knot themselves around unsuspecting hearts. They supposedly traveled in the dark clouds and liked to hide in their shadows. But most of all they loved to play mischievous games of deception and confusion with misguided hearts.

All darkness came from the Land of the Lost beyond the border countries. Every chance they got, these dark spirits infiltrated the kingdom of Christianity and whispered wicked thoughts about the Master, the great and wonderful ruler of all Christianity, to unsuspecting citizens. They especially targeted those living down in the Valley of Despair like Uncle Broken Heart.

In fact, just this morning Hungry Heart's parents had tried to convince Uncle Broken Heart to come back to the Plains of Hope, but he refused. He felt more at home with his friends, Lonely Heart and Empty Heart, than with the folks up on the Plains.

"Hope isn't for me any longer," he told them. "My old eyes can't take the bright sunlight, and you young folks move too fast for me. I'll just stay here till my time comes."

He sat back in his rocking chair and slapped his knees. "Yep, this is home for me now. You go on about your business. You got work to do. I'm gonna wait right here. I got everything I need. Don't need nothin' more and don't want nothin' more."

When the Master asked her parents to remain a few more days to encourage him as well as a nearby family of discouraged hearts, they agreed and sent Hungry Heart back to stay with Grandfather Humble Heart. Her mother urged her to return with two of her cousins, Jealous Heart and Teasing Heart, but she did not look forward to spending the day with them. No, not at all.

"I'll be fine, Mother. The road is clear, and we have plenty of friends along the way. Besides, I have a lot to think about now that you and Father have received your appointments as traveling messengers for the Master. Please let me go by myself."

"Are you sure, Hungry Heart?"

"Oh yes, I'm sure!"

Hungry Heart threw her arms around her parents and gave them each a good-bye hug before she followed the main road that led directly north, up and out of the Valley of Despair.

It wasn't always called the Valley of Despair. Long ago, the Master had set the valley aside and called it the Valley of Restoration. It was a place where wounded hearts could rest and heal. The Master filled the green meadows with colorful wildflowers and channeled mountain waterways into quiet streams. Every day he visited the valley to talk to broken hearts, care for their wounds, and prepare nourishing food for them. He constantly reminded them, "My hope will not disappoint you; my love will not fail you; and my faith will sustain you. People may let you down, but I will not."

The Master never intended for anyone to remain in the valley permanently, but over the years more and more people came down from the Plains of Hope and decided to stay. Before long, they stopped watching for the Master's daily visits. Instead, they found consolation in simply talking to each other about their wounded hearts, their disappointments, and valley life in general. They could spend all day thinking about their troubles instead of encouraging one another. Eventually all hope disappeared from the valley, and it became known as the Valley of Despair. No matter where one went in the valley, someone was always singing the discouraging little valley tune:

What will be will be, so what do you see?
My rainbows are fadin' and my troubles are stayin'.

Thud! All thoughts of the valley fled as Hungry Heart tripped over a tree branch in the middle of the road and landed on her hands and knees. "Oh!" she cried out, startled. Her decision to walk alone back to Grandfather's suddenly seemed unwise. "I should have listened to Mother..."

The words were barely out of her mouth when strong arms pulled her up and she was looking at Grandfather Humble Heart, who had come out to meet her.

"Girl, I've been a'lookin' for you. C'mon, I don't like the looks of this wind. It's a'whippin' up much too fast for us to be out here. There now, you're safe, and you've still got your paradigm pouch, so the important things are taken care of. Let's be goin'."

He wrapped his arm around her shoulders and held her slender body close to his stout frame until they reached his house. Once inside the warmth of the small cottage, Grandfather bolted the door behind them with a satisfied nod and a casual stroke of his long gray beard. For years he had made those motions, a routine ritual, as if to say, "All is well."

Hungry Heart's eyes slowly adjusted to the soft glow that encircled the kitchen table lantern. Outside, a sudden mixture of rain and hailstones attacked the windows with rapid-fire precision. They had made it inside just in time! Grandfather hurried to give his shaking granddaughter a mug of hot chamomile tea. Gently he rested his hand on her trembling fingers for a reassuring squeeze.

"Girl, you're gonna catch a chill. Here now, you drink your tea and I'll fetch somethin' to cover you up with."

He quickly turned into an adjoining room and returned with a thick, crocheted afghan, which he tucked around her shoulders. He watched her shaking subside before he turned away and relaxed—but not before an anxious sigh escaped him. *The wind is growin' stronger every minute. I've never seen anythin' like this. My house is well built, but this is different... Where is the Master?* he thought.

Normally the Master watched over his kingdom with a careful, all-seeing eye. Nothing, absolutely nothing, transpired within its borders without his knowledge. He could travel quickly, in the blink of an eye, to any corner of Christianity at any time, day or night. No concern was too small for his attention. One look from him could still trembling hearts and send disgruntled spirit creatures back to the Land of the Lost. However, more often than not, he simply and quietly made provision or resolved the problem without drawing attention to himself.

Oh, how Grandfather Humble Heart and Hungry Heart needed him now!

Crash! A loud noise against the backside of the house startled both of them. Hungry Heart jumped to her feet. "Grandfather, what...?"

"Just a loose shutter, just a loose shutter...no need to be concerned, child. I've been a'meanin' to fix it. There now, you just come over here and sit down by me. We'll wait this thing out together."

5

Hungry Heart settled beside her Grandfather. "I don't dare imagine what might have happened if you hadn't found me, Grandfather."

"Let's not think about that. If we do, we'll be a'listenin' to the shadows instead of the Master's heart. Besides, I want to show you somethin'."

Reaching into the pouch he carried over his heart, he carefully pulled a miniature ring. Hungry Heart caught her breath.

"It's a new paradigm piece!"

Each time a citizen of Christianity received an impartation of truth from the Master, he or she received a paradigm piece. The Master used refined gold and silver and intricately cut gemstones to create beautiful symbols that could be admired, studied and discussed. His truth endured forever; therefore, these crafted symbols also needed to be able to stand the test of time. Although very precious and often quite ornate, no monetary value was ascribed to them. Each piece existed solely for the Master's purpose. Paradigms and paradigm pieces could not be traded, bought, sold or passed down to family members. Only the Master himself could bestow a paradigm piece, for he alone knew how to fit his truth into each person's life.

Hungry Heart reached out to touch the tiny ring resting in Grandfather's palm. Three gold bands had been braided together and formed into a ring, then polished to perfection. With awe and appreciation in her voice, she repeated the traditional refrain that had been echoed from generation to generation. "Please, tell me the story of this paradigm piece."

Thankful for an opportunity to ignore the howling winds and pelting rain outside, Grandfather Humble Heart cleared his throat and began. His eyes half closed, he waved his arm before him as if seeing the scene unfold once again.

"Just this week, as I was at the top of Faith Mountain, I saw the Master as the all-sufficient one. He is sufficient enough for this here storm. We do not have anythin' to be afraid of because we belong to him. Remember that, Hungry Heart. Wherever you are and whatever is happenin' around you, you belong to the Master. You are a citizen of Christianity. This ring of truth reminds us that he was, he is, and he always will be. He is three in one. He has no beginning, and he will have no end."

Hungry Heart nodded respectfully. She didn't quite understand it, but Grandfather held a paradigm piece of truth in his hand, and if the Master proclaimed truth, then it remained forever. She touched it one more time before Grandfather Humble Heart carefully returned the small ring to the worn leather pouch that held all his paradigm pieces.

Once a citizen received the appointed number of pieces for his life, the Master would carefully fit them together, like intricate puzzle pieces, to form a completed paradigm. Then he would assign that person a "place of appointment" in his service. These carefully sculptured paradigms of truth ranged from the size of a small pearl to that of a large pocket watch. Like beautiful pieces of jewelry, they could be carried in pouches or worn openly.

Despite the number of paradigm pieces bulging from her grandfather's leather pouch, he had not yet received his completed paradigm or his appointment in the Master's service. Still, Grandfather Humble Heart accepted one day at a time and served the Master from his little house by showing concern and hospitality to everyone he met. Although he rejoiced when others completed their paradigm quests, he found his uncomplicated life on the Plains of Hope very fulfilling. Family and friends lived nearby, and his daily routine remained comfortably familiar. He had no desire whatsoever to embark on a paradigm quest of his own.

Besides, taking care of Hungry Heart in her parents' absence gave his own heart a special joy, especially since the Master had called his dear wife Trusting Heart to the highest heavens a few months ago. He missed Trusting Heart a great deal, but he found comfort in knowing that she now enjoyed the greatest gift in all of Christianity: everlasting life and eternal joy.

From time to time, the Master spoke about the life beyond the kingdom of Christianity and the great mansions prepared for everyone. However, if citizens pressed him for more details, he just smiled and assured them, "When the time comes, we'll go together and I'll answer all your questions. Until then, I promise to keep you busy right here."

Since Hungry Heart's parents had received their appointments as traveling messengers for the Master last year, Grandfather and Hungry Heart had spent a great deal of time together. Her long dark hair and hazel eyes reminded him so much of her grandmother, Trusting Heart. The endless questions pouring out of his granddaughter's hungry heart usually kept him busy talking, and he loved to tell a good tale from the Master's Great Book. Today, however, he watched anxiously as she jumped up from her sheltered seat by his side to peer out the kitchen window time and again.

The storm had grown stronger while Grandfather talked. Relentless winds tossed tree branches and debris in every direction. Hungry Heart spoke loudly to make herself heard above the deafening storm.

"Grandfather, where is the Master? Why doesn't he stop this storm? If it reaches the valley, Uncle Broken Heart won't make it! He isn't strong enough to survive. And Mother and Father are down there! Please call the Master to send the wind away...please call Him!"

Grandfather Humble Heart stayed silent. *How can I possibly explain the unexplainable? I've been a'callin' him since the first dark clouds showed up on the plains. Somethin' dreadful musta happened...he just doesn't answer. It's not like the Master...not like him at all.*

His fingers reached up to touch the pouch he carried over his heart. He reminded himself, *He was, he is, and he will be. He is the all-sufficient one. I will not be afraid, and I will not allow fear to take root in my life or in Hungry Heart's life.*

The front door rattled on its hinges, and the bolted latch shook under the pressure from the heavy wind outside. Hungry Heart screamed out in fear just as a large tree branch fell against the window, throwing slivers of glass and cold splashes of rain into the room.

"Grandfather! We will die! What can we do? Oh, Master, where are you? Don't you hear us? Don't you care? We are going to die here!"

Only the thundering wind answered her desperate cries for help. Never, in her entire life, had the Master failed to come immediately when she called. She watched, in shaking silence, as Grandfather tacked up some heavy oilcloth to cover the broken window.

She still stood there when he finished. Taking her by the hand, he led her over to their seat and sat her down next to him. Humming one of their favorite tunes, he tried to remember what the Great Book said about dark storms. Torrential storms like this one used to take place during the Master's reign in the Fatherland. Thousands upon thousands of people had lost everything when the North Wind blew. Legend held that the Master sent all his anger to the Land of the Lost in the North and kept it there— until he saw places that needed to be cleansed from the clutter of man's imagination and selfish plans. Then he sent the North Wind to blow away everything that had been built without his permission.

As much as Grandfather Humble Heart wanted to stay in the cabin close to his granddaughter, a persistent nudge in his heart told him that he had to face the storm in order for it to stop. If he clung to anything at all, it might put his granddaughter in harm's way. No, he had to go out and face this one alone.

"I'm certain the storm will be over very soon, Hungry Heart. C'mon now," he coaxed, wiping a tear trickling down her cheek, "we don't want the Master to find us here all filled with fear and unbelief. Don't be afraid! Be courageous and hopeful!"

Grandfather reluctantly stood up.

"I want you to stay here and wait for me. Keep the lantern lit. I'm gonna find the Master," he said determinedly as he reached in a closet for his coat.

"No! You can't leave me here alone! You can't go out there! Grandfather, the wind will blow you away....and it is so dark....you won't be able to see where you are going. Please don't leave...."

Despite her tearful arguments, he buttoned up his old brown raincoat. Her fear made him more determined than ever to face the perils outside.

"I'm not afraid of the North Wind or of the blasted darkness. Besides, the wind's gonna carry the sound of my voice to the Master, and he's gonna be here in the wink of an eye. Remember my paradigm—he's the all-sufficient one. I'll be back before you know it. I got to go...my heart is tellin' me to go for your sake. Be strong; think hopeful thoughts. Take out your paradigm pieces and hold them close to your heart."

Without giving her an opportunity to respond, he unlatched the door and disappeared into the darkness.

Alone, Hungry Heart clutched her own paradigm pieces against her heart and listened to the North Wind beat against the house like a giant whip. *Where is he? Why isn't he back yet? Where is the Master? What is happening? Will I ever see Mother and Father again?*

Time ticked on. Torrents of rain and hail fell to the ground in sheets while the skies only grew darker. The outside shutters rattled, and the roof creaked with every gust of wind. Minor leaks that Grandfather had intended to fix became major ones as pieces of the roof blew away. Hungry Heart pulled out every bowl and pan she could find to catch the miniature waterfalls. Those cascades joined the streams of tears falling down her cheeks as she continually called, "Master, please come quickly!"

Keeping things dry as best she could, she curled up in Grandfather's favorite chair and pulled her knees tightly up under her chin. She would have to wait out the storm alone. Hungry Heart knew that she should be reciting the paradigm truth she had learned, but the fear in her heart did not leave any room for hopeful thoughts. Preoccupied with her dreadful circumstances, she failed to notice the wisp of darkness slip in through one of the leaks in the roof and cast a shadow over her heart.

Little whispers taunted her. "Hungry Heart, just look at you...why, it looks as if the Master has abandoned you! Didn't he promise to come whenever you needed him?"

"He will come. Something must be wrong. But, he will come," she whispered weakly.

"Perhaps you are no longer good enough for him...do you think?"

More tears poured from her eyes. ·

"What about your grandfather...he's probably lying out there all alone, dying, and it's your fault, you know. If it wasn't for you, this would not be happening...he would be in here, safe and sound."

"Stop!" Hungry Heart cried, throwing both hands over her ears. "Stop! I will not listen to these horrible things! I know they're not true. The Master will come, and Grandfather will be safe...I know...Oh, Master, I need you!"

Even though her hope was weak and faint, it was enough to banish the shadow spirits from her heart.

"Let's get out of here!" the spirit creatures panicked. "If she utters one more word of hope, we shall perish under her feet!"

With that, even before Hungry Heart had time to gather her thoughts, booms of thunder roared through the skies. The crashes sounded, one after another, like a heavenly clock counting off the hour—one, two, three, four, five, six—then complete silence. No more wind, no more rain.

Within moments light filtered through the windows, and Hungry Heart heard sounds of life coming from outside. The storm had passed and, thankfully, she was still alive. Her shaking hands slowly opened the door.

CHAPTER 2

The Aftermath

Speechless, Hungry Heart stood in the open doorway. To her left, down the hill from Grandfather's cottage, stood Mr. Able Heart's house. But she could barely see it through the branches of the uprooted elm tree that leaned precariously against it. On her right, further up the hill, Elder Stubborn Heart's house looked like a woodpile. Wet furniture, broken dishes, clothing, and books littered the once pristine lanes winding through the village. A thick gray mist hovered close to the ground while a few small, dark storm clouds still lingered in the sky.

Hungry Heart watched as friends and neighbors emerged from their homes and began to move silently, slowly, through the ugly sea of broken rubble. Who could comprehend the aftermath of this heartless storm? In a quick motion, she passed her hand over her eyes. What could she do?

"Grandfather! Grandfather! Where are you?" she called. Gingerly she stepped over broken windowpanes and debris, making her way to one person after another. "Have you seen Grandfather Humble Heart?" Some just shook their heads as they continued to sort through their scattered belongings. Others simply ignored her.

Slowly she picked her way through the village. Ahead of her a figure sat in the dirt in front of what used to be a meeting place. *Could that be Grandfather?* But as she hurried forward, she realized that it was Elder Sensible Heart. She stopped in front of him.

His swollen red eyes acknowledged her presence, but he could not speak the unspeakable. His heart was hurting for his precious building that was now reduced to rubble. Hungry Heart sat down beside him for a few minutes, laid her arm on his slumped shoulder, and began patting the back

11

of his tattered green shirt. This man was her father's dearest friend, and he had often helped her make intelligent, sensible decisions.

For years, Sensible Heart studied the Master's Great Book. When the Master appointed him as elder at his meeting place, he renovated the building, started a school for young hearts, and conducted classes every night to teach others how to become elders. Now the building lay in pieces. Yesterday, everything made sense. Today, nothing did.

Two mercy hearts from the meeting place arrived just then, so Hungry Heart kissed the top of Elder Sensible Heart's bald head and stepped away quietly.

No one, it seemed, had escaped the brutal storm. People stumbled around in a state of shock, calling out for family members and for the Master. As Hungry Heart reached the edge of town where several farms sprawled out over the countryside, she saw an elderly man standing, gazing out over the battered cornfields. Though his eyes were tired and sad, they also were filled with questions.

"Who would'a thought that everything could change so fast?" he asked her. "Trouble never gives a warnin' or asks for permission, but it shows up just the same. I've seen a lot a' trouble in my time. Bad times come, and bad times go. I've weathered a lot a' storms, but this one just showed up and snatched up my farm like a hungry buzzard. Some of us have to start all over again. Some will and some won't. Right now, I'm just too old and too tired to think about it…I think I'd best head down to the valley."

Then, anticipating her question before she could ask it, he sighed, "If I see your grandfather on the way, Hungry Heart, I'll tell him that you're a'lookin' for him."

As the day waned, Hungry Heart continued to search. She asked her question of everyone she met, but no one had seen Grandfather Humble Heart. When some of his last words to her—"Be strong; think hopeful thoughts"—came back to her, she tried to obey. She tried to concentrate on hopeful thoughts for him and for the rest of her family.

I will find Grandfather; I know I will. The Master is with him now, and they are on their way to find me. Unfortunately, a sneaking fear in her heart eventually reduced her thoughts to tearful desperation. *I must find him! He has to be all right…what will I do without him?*

By sundown, Hungry Heart was exhausted. When she finally returned to Grandfather's house, several neighbors were sitting on the front porch steps waiting.

"May we sleep here tonight?" Mr. Able Heart asked meekly. "Our houses are gone, and we've no place to go. The North Wind has destroyed everything. Our lives have been shaken and pulled to the ground, just as the Great Book foretold."

"The Great Book foretold? What do you mean? Certainly you don't mean that the Master did this to us? To you? He would never destroy our lives like this—no, never!" Hungry Heart shook her head in disbelief.

Mr. Able Heart managed a slight smile for her sake and laid his bandaged hand on her shoulder. "He has not destroyed our lives, only the things that are not rooted and grounded in his love. Your grandfather served the Master with a humble heart, and he used this house to welcome many strangers. It has been spared...and I am certain that he has been spared also, but so much is gone and so many people are confused."

"The Master must be very angry with someone," Mrs. Self-Righteous Heart interrupted. "This kingdom had better shape up, or there will be more storms to come. I knew it. I just knew something terrible was going to happen sooner or later. People have been testing his patience in more ways than one. I try my best to be a good citizen, but I can't do it alone, you know."

Hungry Heart had heard this little speech before and was not in any mood to hear it again. Grandfather always had such patience with Mrs. Self-Righteous Heart. Hungry Heart had no idea how he could bear to listen to this woman. Her mouth was as large as the enormous colorful hats she wore. Even today, with everyone's lives falling apart, she had one hand clutching that stupid hat as if it was the only thing she had left in the world.

"No, no, this is the work of the spirit creatures from the Land of the Lost. They infiltrated our country because the joyful hearts were not singing loudly enough on the mountains, and now look what's happened," Elder Determined Heart argued.

The scientific hearts blamed the weather patterns while the religious hearts quoted from the Great Book. Children cried for their favorite toys, ignoring the reassurances of their mothers. All in all, the fury of the storm resided in everyone's hearts, and no one seemed to be able to quiet the tempest of opinions.

Hungry Heart wanted to defend the Master again, but she couldn't find the words. So she simply shrugged her shoulders in bewilderment, invited everyone in, and did her best to find enough blankets. When she picked up the afghan Grandfather had wrapped around her shoulders the night before and offered it to a young woman, the woman clasped Hungry Heart's hand with a cry of surprise and joy.

"Hungry Heart, it is you! It's so good of you to let us stay here!"

Hungry Heart stared back at the woman. Recognition came in a flash. This soft-spoken, compassionate-looking young woman was her old friend, Selfish Heart. Normally Selfish Heart could not stop talking about herself or her present personal crisis. However, without another word, Hungry Heart now recognized her friend as "Loving Heart."

A new heart and a new name. This is the way it worked in the kingdom of Christianity. In fact, Elder Determined Heart had been Elder Waffling Heart until the Master sent him to live on Faith Mountain for a year. He used to waver between one decision and another, always changing his mind and constantly needing help to carry out his plans. Now, with his new heart and new name, he stood tall and took charge with strong determination and single-mindedness. Yes, living on Faith Mountain had made a big difference in his life.

Hungry Heart's own name spoke of the treasures in her heart as well. Her incessant hunger to know more pleased all her teachers, and they eagerly fed her their knowledge at every opportunity. Yet, she never seemed to have enough or know enough to satisfy her heart. She longed to complete her paradigm of truth and receive her place of appointment in the Master's service. So she traveled from meeting place to meeting place. There was always "something else" to discover. More often than not, she learned too much for her own good.

Time and time again the elders reprimanded her, "Don't listen to those tales about life beyond the borders of Christianity! Hungry Heart, you must learn to be satisfied with life here. The Master gives us everything we need. It is very dangerous to even think about the border countries."

Their admonishment would help her for a few days. Sooner or later, though, she would hear about the miraculous things happening in the border countries, and life in Christianity seemed boring in comparison. Although she loved the Master, her thirst for knowledge would overtake her, and she would listen to the forbidden stories from the Land of Star Gazing or the Land of Infinite Knowledge.

The elders did their best to teach her, and many hopeful hearts encouraged her over the years. Her parents always smiled and reminded her to be patient, but the desire deep inside her heart continued to cry out for more.

Now, recognizing her old friend, Hungry Heart could barely contain herself. How had Selfish Heart become Loving Heart? Had she received her appointment in the Master's service? Hungry Heart needed to know everything. Questions spilled from her lips like water unleashed from a dam.

"How long has it been? I have missed you so much. Where did you go? I heard rumors that you went to the mountains to live. No one knew where you were. Where were you? What about the storm? How did you manage to escape? "

"Slow down," laughed Loving Heart. "Is everyone taken care of? Then let's go sit over here," Loving Heart gestured to a quiet place in the corner of Grandfather Humble Heart's living room. "I have a great deal to tell you. But first, I want to know about you, my friend. To be honest, you look a little tired—much too tired, in fact. Is there anything that I can do for you?"

Hungry Heart sat with her in the corner, but ignored Loving Heart's question. Instead she continued to pepper her friend with her own questions. "Where were you during the wind? Did you call for the Master? Did you see him? Do you know what has happened? Did you find your family? Have you seen my Grandfather?"

Despite Hungry Heart's pleading eyes and unending questions, Loving Heart could not talk about herself. She felt a deep sense of compassion and concern for her old friend. She was distressed to see Hungry Heart so thin. The dark-circled eyes that pleaded with her almost brought Loving Heart to tears. She gave Hungry Heart a reassuring hug and an encouraging word of hope.

"You need to rest. We'll talk about everything tomorrow while we search for your grandfather."

Weary guests filled all the soft beds and cots, so Hungry Heart and Loving Heart slept on long wooden benches in Grandfather's kitchen porch. He had saved them from an old meeting house years ago and lovingly restored the beautiful oak with Hungry Heart at his elbow. Those days felt so far away as she closed her eyes. *Maybe this is all a bad dream,* she silently hoped. For the first time in her life, her heart ached with the pain of abandonment. *Where has everyone gone? Why didn't the Master come to help? Why did he allow the wind to continue?* For just a moment, she thought she could hear the Master's voice calling from the mountains. But as she strained her ears to listen again, only silence answered.

CHAPTER 3

Celebration and Reunion

The next morning, Hungry Heart woke up to find Loving Heart serving a simple breakfast to the last of the overnight guests. With a fleeting sense of guilt, she thought, *I should be taking care of these people. That's what Grandfather Humble Heart would be doing.* Finally, Loving Heart glanced her way with a big smile.

"Good morning, Hungry Heart. Did you sleep well? How about some nice warm cereal and toast?" Loving Heart set a clean plate on the red-and-white checkered tablecloth and pulled out a chair. "Come on now, eat," she coaxed. "As soon as you finish, we're going to the Celebration."

"The Celebration? Who's having a Celebration? Everyone's homes have been destroyed, and Grandfather's gone. No one knows where the Master is or why he hasn't come to help us. Certainly the Celebration has been canceled, hasn't it?"

Loving Heart pushed back the kitchen curtains to let the morning sunlight in as Hungry Heart sat down to eat. She could tell her friend needed a firm hand this morning.

"No, it has not been canceled, and yes, we are going. We need to go, regardless of whether or not we understand all this. We need to encourage each other to have hope and to help everyone to find their families."

"But..."

Loving Heart took charge with loving-kindness. "No buts. Eat your breakfast. I'll go ahead to see if there's anything the elders need help with. It seems to me that the best way to find your grandfather is by helping others."

Then, with a big smile and a quick reassuring hug, she darted out the door, leaving Hungry Heart alone with her thoughts.

The people of Christianity celebrated the first day of each new week with music, food, entertainment, and good friends. The Celebration gave everyone the opportunity to respond to the Master's love with gestures of affection. Some brought him gifts of food and clothing for the needy hearts. Others gave monetary gifts or offered their talents and time for his service. The elders would tell the Master's story, and sounds of music would ring out from every meeting place, large or small.

Usually Hungry Heart looked forward to the Celebration. Today, however, it seemed quite inappropriate. Everyone had so many personal things to attend to…and besides, she had to find her grandfather. *I'll go for just a little while*, she decided finally, *to see who's there and what's happening. Then I must look for Grandfather.* Hungry Heart splashed some water on her face, brushed her hair as quickly as she could, and dashed out the door, never giving her disheveled clothing a second thought.

Outside, people came from everywhere and gathered along the road. Some mingled and talked while the musicians sang the familiar Celebration songs. Little groups formed around the elders as people turned to them with questions.

Hungry Heart recognized most of the people. Unlike the day before, however, they all looked quite hopeful. How they could be hopeful in such dire straits was beyond Hungry Heart's comprehension. The North Wind had blown away most of the meeting places; those that did remain were sorry sights indeed. So the elders just stopped to speak wherever people wanted to listen.

Hungry Heart watched as families and friends united with joyful hugs. Men slapped each other on the backs and promised to help each other rebuild their homes as soon as possible. Children played and chased their pets from one corner to the next. Surprisingly, the Plains of Hope still echoed with hope.

Hungry Heart passed by one little group after another, pausing just long enough to make certain they were not saying anything she needed to hear. Curious hearts whispered about where the Master might be, but no one questioned his absence out loud. Most of the conversations sounded the same, except for one. Over to the side, a prophetic heart spoke to a few families gathered beneath a large almond tree.

Prophetic hearts did not visit the Plains of Hope on a regular basis. They usually stayed close to the mountains because they liked to see things from a great distance. In addition, the elders often found their messages too harsh for most hopeful hearts. Normally, if anyone wanted to hear a prophetic heart speak, he traveled to the mountains to seek him out.

Today, however, this prophetic heart not only had come down to the Plains of Hope, but he also was speaking publicly! Hungry Heart inched her way closer and sat down behind a large family. His deep full voice commanded attention, so even the children sat quietly beside their parents.

"The Master sent the North Wind to cleanse the Plains of Hope. He sent it to shake everything that can be shaken and to blow away everything that was not rooted in Him. Don't worry about the things that are gone! The Master will rebuild your lives. He is the master builder. He is the one who supplies. He is the one who wants to transform the Plains of Hope into a place that hopes in him."

Hungry Heart listened with all her attention. No one, not even inhabitants from the Mountains of Faith, spoke with such daring boldness. She glanced back over her shoulder, expecting to see one of the elders coming to stop him, but they were so busy answering questions that they failed to notice the little group gathered under the almond tree. The prophetic heart's voice increased in volume.

"Hopeful hearts, listen to me! You have lost your hope in the Master. Your hope has come to depend upon what you possess, who you are, and what you can do. You are becoming self-sufficient hearts, more like the people from the border countries than citizens of the kingdom of Christianity."

Some of the families shook their heads and got up to leave, but the prophetic heart continued, scanning the group until his eyes settled directly on Hungry Heart. Her entire body froze under his gaze.

"If you are hungry to know the truth, you must be willing to pay the price. You must turn aside from the destruction around you and turn to the Master with all your heart. You must journey to the Master's Dwelling on the First Mountain, the Second Mountain, and even the Third Mountain! You must face the fires of the Master's refinery without fear because your hunger will drive you on to find the missing pieces of your paradigm."

The prophetic heart continued speaking about missing paradigm pieces and the mysteries of the Master's Dwelling, but Hungry Heart wasn't listening anymore. The Great Book told that the Master's dwelling covered three entire mountains. During the Fatherland time, people who broke the rules were sent to the First Mountain to work in the Master's refinery, but only his special assistants dared to approach the Second and Third Mountains.

Hungry Heart's heart pounded harder and harder. Surely the North Wind had blown everything away! Her life did lie in pieces around her! Everything and everyone that she had trusted in was gone! She clutched her blue bag tightly. According to this prophetic heart, the missing paradigm pieces could be found only in the Master's Dwelling on the East Mountains. She must find them, regardless of the cost! They held the key to everything she hungered for—her paradigm of truth and her place of appointment in the Master's service. For just a moment, she even forgot about Grandfather. Then her attention was jerked back to the speaker.

"The North Wind has come! Blessed be the Master for sending the North Wind!" As the prophetic heart finished speaking, he nodded and smiled in Hungry Heart's direction before disappearing into the trees. Just as she stood up to run after him, a familiar voice sounded behind her.

"There you are, Hungry Heart! I've been looking everywhere for you."

Hungry Heart spun around at the sound of the beloved voice.

"Grandfather! Where have you been? What happened to you? Did the North Wind blow you far away? Did you find the Master? Have you heard from Mother and Father? Are they safe?"

"Slow down there—one question at a time. Let's walk on back to the house, and I'll tell ya everythin'."

Hand in hand they headed home, waving happily to friends and neighbors to indicate that they had found each other. Suddenly things did not seem so bad after all.

Grandfather Humble Heart took a deep breath, then began to tell his granddaughter, step by step, about his adventure.

"I left the house and started for the road. The wind blew me this way and that till I lost my bearin's. It was impossible to see through the blasted mist, so I kept on a'movin' and eventually the wind died out. I found myself down in the Valley of Despair, not too far from your Uncle Broken Heart's house. I went there straightaway to make certain he and your parents were safe. Yep, they were fine, but so many of the valley people needed help that it was nigh impossible to leave before this mornin'. I knew that you were safe. The Master told me so. You don't need your old grandfather as much as you think you do, you know."

"But where was the Master? Some people are saying that he actually sent the North Wind. What do you think, Grandfather? Do you believe he sent that terrible storm to destroy our village?"

Grandfather Humble Heart stared straight ahead thoughtfully. How could he help his granddaughter to accept what had happened? He knew that, indeed, nothing ever happens in Christianity without the Master's approval—even a storm from the North Wind. He also knew the historical accounts recorded in the Great Book, which told about the Master's releasing the North Wind to cleanse the land.

While he continued to search for exactly the right words, Hungry Heart told him about the prophetic heart and his bold message. After she finished, Grandfather repeated the prophetic heart's last words thoughtfully:

"'The North Wind has come, blessed be the Master for sending the North Wind.' I think that says it all, don't you? The North Wind has come. The Master has sent it. We must thank him for all things, includin' the North Wind. Now it is up to us to find out how he wants to change us. There's no doubt about it—this experience will change all of us, don't you think? Look, we're home. C'mon, I have somethin' to show you."

Once inside the house, Grandfather closed the door and gestured for Hungry Heart to sit down at the table with him. He reached for the small leather paradigm pouch over his heart and pulled something out ever so carefully. Hungry Heart's heart beat faster with excitement.

"Grandfather! Your paradigm! It's complete! You've received your missing pieces! Where? How? Let me see it! Oh, please let me see it!"

Gently he placed the precious paradigm of truth in her hands. Tears filled her eyes as she ran her fingers over the delicate smooth lines. The entire pattern fit in the palm of her hand, yet she could see every finely crafted detail etched on the silver paradigm. A dozen small containers, or vessels, formed a circular wreath around one beautiful cup in the very center, which, like a gentle waterfall, tipped forward slightly to fill the others.

Hungry Heart recognized some of the pieces, but now they were beautiful beyond description and perfectly fitted to each other. She saw branches of wheat engraved on one cup. A delicate cluster of grapes embellished another. Then her eyes focused on a small broken vessel nestled in the circle. Her heartstrings pulled ever so slightly as she identified personally with it. Lifting the paradigm to the sunny window, the reflection from the large center cup gave the surrounding vessels a special vibrancy.

"Oh, Grandfather, it is the most beautiful paradigm I have ever seen." And, following the custom in the kingdom of Christianity that has been practiced since the beginning of time, Hungry Heart repeated the time-honored refrain: "Please, tell me the story."

"The Master's cup overflows to meet every need," Grandfather began. "He is not only the Master, he is also the servant of all. This cup represents the Master's life and these vessels represent the citizens of Christianity. There are many vessels of service in Christianity, but our service to him and to each other is only a reflection of his great love. Each vessel is unique in its own right, yet it is joined with all the other vessels."

"And now," he looked intently into her eyes, "I must serve the Master by goin' back to the Valley of Despair. They are hungry and thirsty people. Their hope is gone. I must give what has been given to me. My cup also runs over because the Master has filled my life with his love and mercy."

Hungry Heart shook her head in protest. "No! Mother and Father are already serving in the valley, and who knows how long they will have to stay there?" At his look, she swallowed her protest, but cried plaintively, "You, too, Grandfather? Have I lost everyone?"

"You are not losin' anyone, Hungry Heart. However, there are things in your life that must go. Your hope is often placed in other people instead of in the Master. Remember the words of the prophetic heart? Your hope must be in the Master alone."

"But you love your life here; I know you do, Grandfather."

"Yes, I do. But I must leave my precious granddaughter and the beautiful Plains of Hope because, if I stay, they'll become more important to me than the Master's service. I know it's a bit much for you to understand right now, but you must try."

Trembling, she reached for his hand and laid the paradigm on his palm. His paradigm message would touch many hearts with the Master's love. In many ways, he had already left, she realized. Instead of fear, a deep sense of peace settled down in her heart. She sighed and relaxed slightly. She could hear the Master softly whispering to her, "I will be with you forever. Do not be afraid."

"I think I do understand, Grandfather. The North Wind has blown upon our lives, and we will never be the same."

Satisfied, Grandfather placed the paradigm of truth in his leather pouch and wrapped his arms around Hungry Heart. It was so very true. Their lives would never be the same again.

CHAPTER 4

Growing Up Is Not Always Easy

The next morning Grandfather packed his copy of the Great Book and a few other things he needed for the Master's service. Hungry Heart encouraged him to take more, but he insisted, "Give everythin' you don't want to a needy heart."

At the door, he turned and gave her a big hug. With a tearful good-bye, Hungry Heart waved at her Grandfather as he started down the path. Although he was glad to be following his Master's will, he didn't want his granddaughter to see his tear-filled eyes.

Hungry Heart slowly closed the door after Grandfather disappeared from sight. Sinking down onto a kitchen chair, she paused to consider her situation.

Mother and Father are serving the Master in the Valley of Despair. Now Grandfather has joined them. It isn't fair. How can I have hope now? Everyone who used to encourage me is gone. I can't find the Master. I know I heard him speak to me, but no one seems to know where he is. Perhaps...perhaps I will have to go to the mountains to find him. Or maybe he is spending his time down in the valley taking care of wounded hearts. What am I to do? Should I stay here to keep Grandfather's house open for needy hearts? But all my friends moved up to the Mountains of Faith. Perhaps I should join them? Oh, Master, where are you and what should I do now?

Instinctively she reached for her blue bag and poured out her paradigm pieces, hoping against hope to see her own paradigm take shape. But it was not finished yet. She still needed more pieces. Disappointed, she gathered them up, put them back in the bag, and stared out the window.

Hungry Heart's eyes fell on a large group of helpful hearts next door busy cutting Mr. Able Heart's old elm tree into firewood.

It was kind of a funny sight. Mr. Able Heart always thought he could do anything and everything, completely by himself. Now he was accepting help from his neighbors. That old tree had turned his life upside down; he realized that he wasn't quite as able as he used to be.

Mrs. Self-Righteous Heart stood right there beside them, wagging her finger and babbling on about the Master's wrath, while a couple of curious hearts watched her. She still had her big hat on her head, but it was a bit weather-beaten now, letting her bright red hair fall down over her shoulders. Some dogs started barking at her, and a few mischievous heart children threw handfuls of small sticks at her, but she kept on ranting and raving. Her voice grew more shrill and loud until quite a crowd had gathered to watch the spectacle.

Even with the noisy neighbors outside, Hungry Heart felt quite alone.

Growing up in Christianity meant certain changes. The passage from childhood to young adulthood varied from one heart to another. Mature hearts generously shared their wisdom and encouragement during young hearts' early years. Parents, grandparents, aunts, uncles, and family friends formed close-knit circles of security and hope. However, as the mature hearts received their appointments, they entrusted the younger ones to the Master's watchful eye. As a result, the circle of hearts around the young hearts usually grew smaller and smaller as time passed.

Normally, in the absence of family and friends, young hearts simply called on the Master and learned to follow his instructions. Today was not a normal situation, though, and Hungry Heart was not happy at finding herself to be quite alone in the aftermath of the North Wind. As she sat and thought, she faced her growing dependence on others for the first time. Her thoughts raced until a name settled in her heart: Loving Heart. *I must find her,* thought Hungry Heart. *Perhaps she can help me.*

Immediately putting action to words, Hungry Heart left the house to look for her friend. Within only a few minutes, she saw Loving Heart seated on a large rock near the remains of a former meeting place, telling a small group of children about the Master. As Hungry Heart approached, she finished her story and sent the children off to tell their parents about the Master's love.

"Hungry Heart, I'm so glad to see you," smiled Loving Heart. "You found Grandfather, didn't you? I saw the two of you going home yesterday. Isn't it wonderful? See, you did have something to celebrate after all!"

Hungry Heart just nodded with a half-hearted smile, unable to admit that as soon as she found her Grandfather, she had lost him again. Loving Heart sensed something amiss and tactfully communicated her concern by referring to the children.

"Did you see all the children here? They need to be reassured that the Master loves them because everything and everyone is in such a state of confusion right now. Come, sit down with me. Some giving hearts baked these pastries—here, they're still warm. Help yourself."

Hungry Heart shuffled her feet nervously in the long grass as she ate the warm, fruit-filled pastry. Loving Heart wore crisp clean clothing, and her feet were covered with clean new sandals. By contrast, Hungry Heart's own shoes were worn out from traveling from meeting place to meeting place and noticeably soiled from the dusty roads. Self-consciously, she pulled them back underneath her threadbare skirt, hoping that Loving Heart had not noticed them. A heart's clothing did not make a fashion statement in Christianity, but it did reflect one's service or lack thereof.

Her own heart seeped in self-pity. *It isn't fair,* she thought. *I've been to every meeting place and listened to so many elders, yet here I am alone, almost in rags, hungrier for truth than ever before, and without my paradigm. I've always done my best to please the elders. But here's Loving Heart, who has lived most of her life quite selfishly. Just look at her! Why, she's beautiful! It's not fair!*

Loving Heart tried not to notice the obvious jealousy directed her way, and after awhile she grew silent. Finally Hungry Heart stopped thinking about herself long enough to ask,

"What has happened to you? Your selfish heart is gone, and you have a new name. You're dressed for the Master's service, and everything you say reflects his love. Did you go to the Mountains of Faith?"

"Yes, I have a new heart and a new name; but no, I did not receive it on the Mountains of Faith. Instead my selfish heart drove me to the very borders of Christianity. I nearly crossed over to find a new life in the Land of Wealth. I wanted to get as much for myself as I could without being concerned for what others need."

Hungry Heart could hardly believe her ears. "No, you didn't...you couldn't...did you?"

"Oh yes, I very nearly did. I was so afraid of losing what I had that I traveled closer and closer to the border. The more I tried to keep for myself, the more I lost. Twice I completely forgot where I hid my things, and once robbers slipped in over the border and stole all my food. The situation just became worse and worse until it seemed that the only way out was to leave Christianity altogether. The Land of Wealth did not seem any worse in comparison to my attempts to live a selfish life in the Master's domain."

"But what happened? You're here now, and with a new heart. What happened—please tell me everything!"

"Well," Loving Heart said, "I had my small bags packed—at least what I had left—and I waited for nightfall to slip over the border. I had started to eat my last piece of bread when an old man came and sat down beside me. He was a very needy heart. Everything about him cried out with emptiness, hunger, loneliness, and disappointment. I don't know how he had managed to travel so far from the Valley of Despair. I continued to eat my bread while he watched me. I didn't think I had enough to share, so I didn't. I tried to convince him to come with me over the border, but he refused, saying that he would rather die a needy heart than to leave the Master.

"When he said that, his eyes became mirrors, and I saw the selfishness of my own heart. I realized that his love for the Master far exceeded anything that I could ever hope to possess. I looked at the small piece of bread in my hand and offered it to him. He reached out to take it with a smile and then disappeared! From that moment on, I have not been the same. The Master completed my paradigm and called me to share the story of his love here on the Plains of Hope."

"Your paradigm? You mean you have it—your very own paradigm of truth? I knew it! I just knew it! May I see it?"

"Of course," Loving Heart smiled. She reached for her neckline and gently pulled out a jeweled necklace. Deep blue, red and purple stones formed clusters of grapes, which hung on delicate silver branches on a golden vine. At first it looked like something that a wealthy heart might wear, but its beauty far surpassed any ornamental jewelry that Hungry Heart had ever seen. Clearly the Master himself had crafted it. Breathless, Hungry Heart could barely utter the traditional, time-honored refrain: "Please, tell me the story."

Loving Heart shared her life-message, the story of the Master's love as the source of all true love. "His love grows in our lives like fruit on a vine.

Fruit is for others, to give away in season. These colors—red, blue and purple—represent the different aspects of his love for us and the different stages of growth in our hearts. The branches are like little hands reaching out with his love. See, the vine and the branches are so intertwined and perfectly blended together that it is impossible to see where the vine ends and the branches begin. His love has completed my life, and I have found all that I have been searching for—and more—in him."

Hungry Heart listened intently as Loving Heart described each detail. When the story ended, Hungry Heart's eyes filled with tears.

"I want the Master's love to grow in my heart like a golden vine also. My hungry heart is just as bad as your selfish heart was because I am always thinking about what I need instead of what others need. I am truly a wretched person, undeserving of the Master's love. It is no wonder that I do not see him or hear him like others do."

Loving Heart gently placed her arms around her friend and gave her a little squeeze of reassurance.

"One thing I have learned, my friend, is that we must follow the path that is before us. I needed to follow my selfish heart to the foot of the border countries, for it was there that the Master met my need. You, too, must follow the hunger in your heart and go where it takes you, because it is there that the Master will meet your need. Where is your heart calling you to?"

Hungry Heart hesitated. Dare she repeat the words spoken by the prophetic heart? In spite of her doubt, her friend's compassionate gaze gave her the courage to speak without fear.

"I want to find the Master's Dwelling Place on the First, Second and Third Mountains. I want to know why the North Wind came to blow everything out of my life. I want to find my missing paradigm pieces and serve the Master. I want to know where I belong in the kingdom of Christianity. I want to…oh, I just want to know…and the hunger is so deep inside me that the elders' words do not reach it any longer. What do you think, Loving Heart? Do I dare go? I do not know anyone who has been to the Master's Dwelling. Is it safe to go?"

"I don't know," Loving Heart replied. "But I do know this. If you stay here, you will die of hunger. If you go, you will die to your hunger, just as I died to my selfishness."

CHAPTER 5

Campfires and Traveling Hearts

Stealing just a few more moments under the cozy quilts in Grandfather's big feather bed, Hungry Heart replayed every detail of yesterday's conversation. Loving Heart had agreed to go as far as the First Mountain with her today. But the longer Hungry Heart thought about it, the more she questioned her decision.

Should I try to reach the Third Mountain? What if the journey is too long and too hard for me? Will Mother and Father understand?

Just then a still small voice deep inside her heart spoke.

"Hungry Heart, this is what you have been longing for."

Encouraged, Hungry Heart threw back the covers and got up to prepare for her journey. She gathered her things and hurried to meet Loving Heart. The two friends did not waste much time but immediately began their journey.

Soon Hungry Heart and Loving Heart found themselves leaving the well-traveled roads for narrow footpaths. Sometimes the trail almost disappeared from sight! Nevertheless, Loving Heart appeared to know the way, so Hungry Heart followed her closely.

After taking one particular sharp turn, the path suddenly came out on an open road. From this road they could see an enormous campground at the bottom of the hill.

"Loving Heart, what is this? Why, there must be hundreds, no, thousands of tents here. Where did all these people come from?"

"This is the Campground of Christianity. These people have come from everywhere—from the plains, the cities, the mountains, and even from the border countries. They all have come to meet the Master, many of them for the first time."

"Meet him? Why? Everyone in Christianity already knows who the Master is. Why are they camping here to meet him?"

"Hungry Heart, there are many different ways to know someone. Not everyone knows the Master in quite the same way. These people are searching for something, and this is part of their search. Don't be so quick to judge them for not seeing the Master the same way you see him. They've made it here, to the foot of his Dwelling Place. For now, this is a good place for them. Many of these people are still living under the old rules. Some have escaped from painful lives in the border countries."

Hungry Heart lowered her head in shame. These people had all followed their hearts in different ways, for different reasons, and across different paths, just as she had. Now they were all here together.

"Are they all going to the Third Mountain?" she asked quietly.

"Oh no," Loving Heart answered. "Most will be content to go to the First Mountain to enter the Master's Dwelling. Some will continue over the Second Mountain, but only a few will go to the Third Mountain. Actually," she paused, "there are many who will never go any farther than this campground."

"No further than this? Then why even come?" queried Hungry Heart incredulously.

"Because they are following their hearts, just as you are doing. The distance they travel is not important. Listen to me carefully, Hungry Heart. How far you go is not important; why you are going is."

All the while Loving Heart and Hungry Heart had been talking, they had been descending the hill to the camp. Now, on the outskirts, they passed a family of weak hearts gathered around their campfire. Hungry Heart smiled politely and tried to keep walking, but Loving Heart stopped as the father's eyes met hers.

"How far have you traveled, Mr. Weak Heart?"

"From deep in the valley," the man replied. "Took us nearly a month to reach this place, what with our weak hearts and all. It isn't what we expected, but we're here now and we'll just make the best of it for as long as we can."

"How did you manage such a distance? Did you walk the entire way?" asked Hungry Heart, curious.

Most citizens did walk from place to place, unless the Master provided them with some other means, like a horse or a carriage. Life in the kingdom of Christianity existed for only one purpose—to serve the Master and to care for one another. A fast paced, pressure-filled way of life belonged elsewhere, not in the Master's domain.

"Feet were made for walking," the older folks said. "They get us where we need to go or we don't need to be there." During the past few years, the number of carriages had increased in the cities, but walking gave one time to consider life, concentrate on the journey, and visit with other travelers. Weak hearts, however, usually took longer to complete their journeys because they needed so much rest along the way. As a result, very few weak hearts left their hometowns at all.

The man answered Hungry Heart's question. "Well, yes, we did a bit of walking. In fact, we walked most of the time, except for the last few miles when some mercy hearts had enough room in their wagon for us. Trouble is, there's too many of us for just anyone to make room for."

And that there were, for a tribe of children scrambled out of the worn tent, crying for their mother and teasing each other. Embarrassed, Mrs. Weak Heart tried to settle them down and apologized for their unruly behavior.

"How many children do you have?" Hungry Heart asked as she tried to count the constantly moving heads.

"Twelve, so that makes fourteen of us all together." Mrs. Weak Heart waved her hand over the lot. "Most of us are ailing in one way or another. The children all have weak hearts, too. I don't like to complain, but life hasn't been easy. We probably should have stayed in the valley, but we heard that the Master had this place here where weak hearts could be changed into strong hearts. We just had to try." Tears appeared at the corners of her sad eyes.

"No, you did the right thing," Loving Heart assured her. "You came to the right place for the right reason. This is the place where weak hearts find the strength to go on."

Mrs. Weak Heart smiled limply and brushed away the strands of loose hair falling in her face. One of the youngest cried for a story and pulled at her skirt, so she herded as many as she could over to the campfire to sit down with her.

The father just shook his head in bewilderment. "I've spent my entire life trying to find the Master in the valley, and I've always missed his visits. Now that we're here, they tell me that we have to go up the First Mountain to find him. Momma says she just can't make it with the children and all. It would be wrong for me to leave them here like this while I try to find my own way. After all, I am their father, and they depend on me."

"Perhaps you've already found your way?" Loving Heart suggested to him with a knowing smile.

"Nope, I don't know where I'm headed. I haven't a clue what I should do from here."

"If you have come to the end of what you can do and how far you can go, then this is the place where the Master will meet you."

Mr. Weak Heart let out a deep breath. "Are you saying that I can just wait for him to find me here?"

"Look over there—I think he already has…"

Loving Heart pointed just beyond the campfire where the Master now sat talking to Mrs. Weak Heart and the children. Both Hungry Heart and Mr. Weak Heart stared at them in disbelief before it all started to sink in. As soon as the father collected himself, he ran over to them, calling joyfully, "Momma, Momma, he's found us! He's found us!"

Just as excited to see the Master after such a long time, Hungry Heart stepped forward to join them. Loving Heart moved in front of her and blocked the way.

"No, Hungry Heart. This is not your campfire or your need. This is not the Third Mountain, is it? This is their time, and it's time for us to go."

Reluctantly, Hungry Heart nodded. She followed Loving Heart deeper into the sea of tents and makeshift lean-tos.

Off to one side, a group of enthusiastic hearts was stirring up a camp-fire for some traditional hearts, but more than coals were getting stirred up.

"No, no, you don't do it like that! Here, the stick goes in this way…" one older gent declared, grabbing the stick himself to take over.

"But it will burn faster if you do it this way!" the young enthusiastic heart said.

"This is the way we have always done it here. You go make your own camp if you can't listen to us. We like it our way! This is the way the Master wants campfires built here. You just go ask him yourself if you don't believe me! You young folks are all alike, never willing to listen to anything."

Hungry Heart and Loving Heart just nodded quickly at the group and kept on moving. Up ahead, two enormous fires were burning. It looked as though someone was in trouble! Rushing forward, they found themselves standing between two separate camps of competitive hearts. Each group was trying to build the biggest and brightest fire. Men scrambled for more wood, and women fanned the flames with large leafy branches. Catching sight of Hungry Heart and Loving Heart, everyone called out at once from both directions,

"Over here! Come over here to help us! Help us make our fire bright enough for the entire campground to see! Then the Master will be most pleased with us!"

"No! Come over here! We have wood that will burn through the night. Their fire will be gone in a few hours because they don't know what they are doing!"

Before Loving Heart and Hungry Heart could respond, a reckless heart came running between the two fires. Her long full skirt caught fire and threw sparks in every direction, nearly setting a nearby tent on fire. One of the older women pulled her to the ground and beat the flaming skirt until the fire went out. Thankful, the reckless heart apologized for the intrusion and promised to be more careful. Before the reckless heart left, Loving Heart called her aside and gently explained how dangerous it was to run from place to place. Hungry Heart just stood and watched the comedy before her.

When Loving Heart and Hungry Heart moved away from the scene a few minutes later, they noticed a young couple sitting off by themselves, looking quite forsaken. They were divided hearts; such hearts were always miserable. Differences would set in between family members—differences that often appeared irreconcilable—and send them down to the Valley of Despair. Although the elders tried to teach everyone how to live together in peace and harmony, sometimes hearts just refused to live together according to the Master's Great Book. At that point, only the Master himself could change their hearts and give them new names.

"Excuse me, please," Loving Heart asked courteously, to begin conversation, "we are on our way to the gate. Would you like to join us?"

The young man looked up. "She can go with you if she wants to, but I've decided to go back home. This journey is ridiculous. If the Master didn't change her heart at home—where she belongs, I might add—then what makes her think that he will change it out here in this wilderness?"

The young woman shifted a bit further away from her husband and tried to apologize for his rude behavior.

"Please forgive us, but I don't think we would make very good traveling companions. As you can see, it is difficult, if not impossible, for us to agree on anything any longer. I had hoped that we could journey to the Second Mountain together because I've heard that miracles take place there; but if he won't go, he won't go."

"No, I won't go," the young man grumbled. "I'm tired of your endless nagging about the Second Mountain. It's all a bunch of superstition anyway! I've had it!"

"It's not superstition! It's written in the Great Book and taught by the elders. The Master disapproves of separation between hearts, and he wants us to…"

"Yeah, yeah, he wants us to…that's all I ever hear anymore. Well, you go ahead and find out what he wants. I'll be at home. If and when you ever decide to come back, you know where to find me."

With that he plopped his hat on his head, turned around and began trekking home, leaving his young wife sobbing uncontrollably.

Hungry Heart tugged at Loving Heart's sleeve and started to fire hushed questions at her.

"What should we do? Should we take her with us? Do you know what to say to make her feel better? Should we go after him and try to make him change his mind? We can't just leave her here all alone, can we?"

Loving Heart shook her head. "Sometimes the only thing we can do is to give each heart the freedom to follow his own journey. We have to set aside our feelings for such hearts and trust the Master. He has placed a journey before them, but it will be up to them to accept or reject it. As much as we want to help her, this girl needs time to decide what the Master wants her to do."

Loving Heart sighed and motioned for Hungry Heart to join her as they walked away quietly.

Aside from these few encounters, their journey through the campground proved to be relatively peaceful. But the closer they came to the First Mountain, the less Loving Heart spoke. She continued to smile and touch Hungry Heart's hand with reassurance from time to time, but she wanted to give her friend every opportunity to contemplate her own journey.

By sundown, Hungry Heart could see, in the distance, a large stone archway that marked the gate to the First Mountain.

"Look!" she exclaimed, clutching at Loving Heart's arm. "There's the gate!"

"I see it," she said, and stopped short. "Hungry Heart, this is as far as I go. This is your journey now."

At first Hungry Heart tried to persuade her to continue, but Loving Heart remained determined to go back to the Plains of Hope. So Hungry Heart gave her good friend a warm hug.

"Good-bye, Loving Heart," she said. "Thank you so much for all your help and encouragement."

Loving Heart smiled, squeezed her friend again, and turned to go.

Hungry Heart resolutely faced the gate and started forward. After traveling alone a few hundred yards, the wind started to blow. Within a few short minutes, pelting rain and hail forced her to seek shelter under the cleft of a large rock. Soon sheets of water poured from the sky.

When the storm stopped an hour or so later, Hungry Heart breathed a sigh of relief. Carefully she climbed up on the wet rock to rest and try to dry herself in the sun peeking through the clouds. A kind-looking gentleman sitting just a few feet away nodded to her.

"You brought quite a storm with you, young lady."

"Sir, I didn't bring it. I had nothing to do with this storm," Hungry Heart's eyebrows rose in surprise.

When the man simply smiled, she immediately recognized him as a wisdom heart. One hardly ever, if ever in fact, met more than one or two wisdom hearts in a lifetime. There weren't very many of them because it took so many years to attain hearts of wisdom. Instantly, a pang of remorse struck her for daring to rebuff a wisdom heart.

"I am so sorry. Please forgive me. I meant to say, 'How did I bring the wind?'"

"No, no, you said what you meant. Always say what you mean and mean what you say. Anything else will lead to conversations that don't mean anything."

Hungry Heart nodded, then took advantage of his presence to inquire, "But, pray tell, where exactly did the storm come from?"

"The tempest came with you. It is the chaos of your life, a storm of confusion beating against the hunger in your own heart. Your hungry heart has led you this way and that. You have searched in many places and tasted many things, my dear. Chaos follows you wherever you go, and it will continue to do so until your hunger is satisfied. Your life is in pieces because you do not see the beginning from the end."

Hungry Heart listened intently to his words. It was true that her constant hunger for new experiences had taken her to many places. She had been to the retreats on the Mountains of Faith many times and collected paradigm pieces. (The mountain teachers always loved to see hungry hearts come because they listened so intently.) She knew every meeting place in Christianity and often spent time with the elders. It did not matter whether they talked quietly or loudly, or with simple or complicated terms, Hungry Heart felt at home every time she went.

Hungry Heart felt for her bag of paradigm pieces. How could this wisdom heart call the pieces of her life "chaos" and insinuate that they had caused that violent storm? Yet, he was a wisdom heart. Therefore, Hungry Heart received his words, thanked him for his counsel, and hopped off the rock to continue her journey.

PART TWO
THE
First Mountain

CHAPTER 6

Through the First Gate

$\cdot\!\!-\!\!\bullet\!\cdot\!\bullet\!\cdot\!\!-\!\!\cdot$

Smiling broadly, Hungry Heart picked her way through the rocks to join a stream of people heading for the wide stone archway marking the gate to the First Mountain. Men, women, children—hearts of every description—moved together in unison. All carried the same thought in their hearts. At last, my journey to the Master's Dwelling begins.

"Hello, Hungry Heart! I am so glad to see you here."

Hungry Heart spun around to see a sacrificial heart smiling at her.

"The Master has assigned me to be your traveling companion. Come on! Let's join the others."

True to her nature, Hungry Heart began pelting her new companion with questions as they moved closer to the group gathering in the gateway. She asked so many, in fact, that Sacrificial Heart interrupted her firmly.

"Hungry Heart, I do not know where the rest of your paradigm pieces are, and I do not know how long this journey will last. I do know that your heart must begin to learn the discipline of quiet stillness. Sometimes it is necessary to sacrifice the desire of the moment for the greater truth."

A little embarrassed, yet intrigued with the promise of "a greater truth," Hungry Heart bit her tongue and stopped talking. They waited quietly with the other people until a white-robed man motioned for the group to sit down in the archway. To her surprise, it was wide enough to accommodate everyone, stretching out like an enormous umbrella. Long red, blue, purple, and white banners hung overhead, bringing a festive and joyful atmosphere to the occasion. Hungry Heart strained to see to the far side of the crowd, but there were just too many people.

After everyone settled underneath the colorful flags waving gently in the wind, the man started to speak. "You have been invited here by the Master for a specific purpose. He opens the door of his Dwelling Place to you because he loves you. However, he wants you to know that you are about to embark on a journey that will change you forever. So first I must ask you some questions. Do you love the Master? Are you willing to affirm your love for the Master in the presence of one another? Do you promise, to the best of your ability, to love him with your whole heart, as well as to love one another during this journey?"

Nearly everyone nodded their heads or said "yes" to his questions. The zealous hearts shouted their affirmative answers loudly enough for everyone to hear while a few curious hearts glanced at one another with a quizzical look. One young man, after a long pause, shook his head sadly and got up to make his way back to the campground. Hungry Heart stared after him, but Sacrificial Heart caught the look in her eyes and whispered quietly, "It is not his time."

Hungry Heart turned her attention back to the white-robed man. By now she recognized him as one of the Master's assistants. It was his job to serve at the gate. She listened closely for his next instructions.

"Please lay aside everything that will encumber your journey or that might hinder someone else. Do not take any thought for your food or clothing. The Master will provide everything you need. Please respect the Master's authority in all things and do not go beyond the appointed path."

Hungry Heart looked down at the little satchel clutched in her hand. It held a few personal items from home—her treasured books, a notebook, pens, a change of clothing, and some snacks. She looked up to see others depositing their extra food and clothing at the gate. But Hungry Heart saw no harm in taking her few things. After all, they could be carried with one hand. Sacrificial Heart waited quietly for Hungry Heart to make up her mind. After it was obvious that the bag was going to remain on Hungry Heart's arm, they stepped through the archway.

The brilliantly colored banners waving in the breeze above them gradually lengthened until they touched the travelers' heads. As the people continued forward, the soft, linen banners brushed against their faces and eventually reached to their knees. A dazzling kaleidoscope of red, blue, purple, and white fabric draped their shoulders in royal splendor and ushered them through the gate. Hungry Heart could hardly believe the glory of it all as the fabric brushed against her body like a gentle spring wind. She felt like a princess, dressed for the ball.

On the other side, a myriad of new sights, sounds, and smells greeted everyone. One image after another drew Hungry Heart's attention until she felt dizzy. Just when she thought she'd fall over, someone nearby touched her shoulder.

"Steady there, Hungry Heart. Don't try to take it all in at once. That's too much for even the strongest of hearts."

Hungry Heart spun around to face another white-robed assistant.

"You have entered the First Mountain of the Master's Dwelling Place, and I want to tell you that time is measured quite differently here."

She opened her mouth to speak, but he continued without giving her a chance to interrupt.

"The Master is all and in all. He is the beginning and the end. He lives in the past, in the present, and in the future. Everything that ever has happened, is happening, or will happen within his Dwelling Place is taking place at the same time. Do you understand?"

His words sounded more like a riddle than an explanation. Her puzzled look answered for her.

"No, of course you don't, but you will. Be patient. Don't worry. You will see time pass just as you always have. The sun will rise and set because your body needs to rest and your mind needs time to reflect. The Master knows this. Step slowly and do not miss anything in front of you. Keep your eyes straight ahead and focused on the Master. You will see many people and many things to your right and to your left, but if you stop to investigate each one, you will lose your bearings. Stay focused, and always remember this: It is not how far you go that matters, but why you are going."

Upon hearing this reminder again, Hungry Heart reached to pull out her notebook and write it down. When she looked up, the assistant had disappeared into a large sea of people, all dressed in the same soft white linen robes. She tried to steal another quick look around her, but found herself getting dizzy again. Snippets of conversations and recountings of the Master's story in hundreds of different ways floated to her ears. Images and voices blended together in a whirlwind of time and space around Hungry Heart. Then, like a drowning man clutching at a lifeline, she closed her eyes to remember the assistant's words. When she opened them again, Sacrificial Heart stood by her side, looking straight ahead.

Hungry Heart followed Sacrificial Heart's gaze. Four wide stone steps led, at least as far as she could see, to a large dark tunnel leading inside the mountain itself.

"Sacrificial Heart, I'm supposed to go up the mountain, not through it. There must be some mistake."

"There's no mistake. This is the Master's path for you. This tunnel leads through the mountain catacombs and up to his refinery."

"To th...the...refinery? You mean the Master's Great Refinery?" In spite of herself, Hungry Heart's voice caught on the last word.

"Yes, we have to hurry now. Look, the last of our group is leaving."

"But, wait! I am going to the Master's Dwelling, not the refinery. People from the Fatherland who broke the rules—they went to the refinery. There must be some mistake. I haven't broken any rules...I have lived in Christianity all my life..."

"There is no mistake," said Sacrificial Heart quietly.

"There must be. I can't go to the refinery, I just can't."

"Do you want to go back?"

"No, I want to go up the mountain. I just don't want to go this way. Please, can't we find another way?"

"This is the way, but the choice is yours." Sacrificial Heart fell silent and waited.

Hungry Heart battled with her fear.

"I can't go back, but I can't stay here forever. I may be crazy, but I've got to keep going," she finally sighed.

Despite Hungry Heart's misgivings, she bit her lip and braced herself like a child waiting for a dreaded punishment. They stepped into the tunnel at the end of the line and followed the orderly procession. Quietly they walked through miles of narrow mountain passages, occasionally stopping for a sip of water from the natural springs in the rock bed. All along the way, travelers discarded their bags and parcels. Determined to keep hers, Hungry Heart shifted it from arm to arm and kept moving.

By the time they reached daylight again, the afternoon sun stood high in the sky. After walking in dimness for so long, Hungry Heart had to pause and let her eyes readjust to the light. When she focused on the sight in front of her, Hungry Heart's knees went weak. A large deep crater lay in the middle of the mountain! Blazing flames and heavy smoke reached into the sky from the core, a bubbling lake of red and yellow molten fire. Never, in her wildest fantasies, had she envisioned the refinery like a volcano ready to spew molten lava everywhere! Terrified, she panicked. "There must be some mistake! Sacrificial Heart, please, let's go back. Please, take me home."

This time Sacrificial Heart ignored the request. Instead she wisely addressed the fear behind Hungry Heart's plea to go back.

"Don't be afraid, Hungry Heart. The Master has watched over this refinery fire for many generations. We are quite safe, I assure you. Listen, over there is one of the Master's assistants telling the story of the great fire."

Trembling, Hungry Heart's eyes never left the column of fire and smoke in the distance as she sat down on the warm ground to listen. She constantly scooted around in an attempt to find a cooler seat. Beads of sweat covered her forehead. Everyone around her seemed to be equally apprehensive. A few mothers gathered up their children and headed back toward the tunnel until one of the assistants stopped them.

"Please, do not be afraid. The Master has made provision for you and the children. He knows exactly what you need. Trust him to supply."

Hungry Heart knew that the Great Book described the Master's refinery fire. She also had heard many of the legends that revolved around it, most of which she had chosen not to believe. After all, no one had ever shown her a paradigm describing the refinery.

Sometimes, at night when the sunset glowed with red and orange hues, Grandfather would lean back on his porch rocker and say, "See, the Master's fire burns day and night to remind everyone of his triumph over his enemies. The fire in our hearts must never go out, Hungry Heart, it must never go out…"

Up until now, his words had little relevance for her life. *Could this*, she wondered, *be the very same fire Grandfather used to point to in the sky?* The assistant's voice interrupted her memories. The mountain crater naturally amplified his voice.

"A long time ago, the Master used to live far away from the people, here at his Dwelling Place, which still covers the three highest mountains in Christianity. He visited the people from time to time and gave them many rules to keep—a long list of laws and duties required for citizenship. These rules provided a way for them to maintain proper standards of conduct as well as to pay their citizenship taxes. If they kept the rules, they were awarded many rights and privileges.

"The Master assigned assistants to ensure that the rules were followed correctly. When the people broke the rules, they became indebted to the Master's service. So the Master provided a way for those who broke the rules to pay the penalty of taxation, yet continue to live in the land. He allowed them to come here, to his refinery, for short periods of time to work off their debts. This may seem cruel to you, but he did it because he loved the citizens and wanted them to learn to live together peacefully.

"Eventually the assistants added more and more rules, with the result that fewer and fewer people were able to keep them. They raised the taxes so high that only the rich could afford them. In doing so, they broke the rules themselves. In fact, the assistants were so busy counting the tax collections that they neglected the refinery fires and allowed them to die out.

"Over time the people stopped caring about the Master. They lived selfishly and sometimes very wickedly. Their indebtedness grew larger and larger. They stopped coming to the Master's refinery. They did not understand that his love for them burned as deeply and as profoundly as the mountain fire itself. Neglected love becomes jealous love, and jealous love eventually becomes wrath. After years of neglect, his refinery fire erupted in fury, flowed down the mountainside and consumed everything in its path. The catacomb tunnels you passed through today are a result of that eruption. The fiery lava literally cut its way through the mountain.

"The people ran to the Mountains of Faith and cried out to the Master for help. From the beginning, the Great Book explains, the Master planned to come and help them. Now he left the mountain to spend some time living among the people.

"This made quite a stir. His assistants got quite upset because he did not interpret the rules the same way that they had been interpreting them for the people. In addition to everything else, he appeared to neglect his assistants and spent most of his time on the street listening to common complaints. As a result, the assistants plotted to overthrow their Master in the Great Revolt.

"When the Great Revolt took place, the Master's assistants killed him. A few faithful servants brought his body here, to his own refinery, and buried him in one of the catacombs. What happened then is a great and awesome mystery. The fire in the refinery burned until it became white-hot, hotter than ever before.

"Darkness covered the land as the sun disappeared from the sky. The rebellious assistants celebrated their victory and made plans to control the Fatherland. People ran and hid in their homes for three days—when something miraculous happened. A brilliant light filled the land, a light more radiant than the sun itself. The Master returned, alive, and stronger than ever!

"The Master actually came back to life and walked out of the catacombs with his eyes blazing like fire! After he proclaimed everyone's debts to be paid in full, he reclaimed his throne and established a new decree over the land: 'Free citizenship to all believing hearts.' Today he sits on a throne of fire on the Third Mountain to remind his enemies that he will live forever!

"After the Great Revolt, the Master opened up this refinery again. Although citizenship in Christianity is now free, and there are no more debts to pay, he offers everyone the opportunity to serve at the refinery. Years ago men and women came here to pay their debts. Today, you come here to express your inexpressible love for the Master. Some of you are searching for paradigm pieces, others are seeking your place of appointment, and many of you are here because, quite simply, there is no place else to go.

"It is here that the Master refines the precious truth for your paradigm pieces. His truth is forged in the fire seven times to make certain that it is pure. Afterwards it is molded, shaped and polished to perfection. Our eyes see gold and silver, but they are only a natural reflection of his eternal truth. He uses the common things of this world to communicate the uncommon.

"This fire burns day and night to remind people everywhere of his love. For those who have eyes to see, this pillar of fire and the column of smoke can be viewed from any place in the Kingdom of Christianity.

"Thank you for coming. I know that you will be of great service to the Master. You each will be given an assignment specifically suited for your journey. Always remember, you have come of your own free will and you may leave at any time if you perceive that the journey is too difficult."

CHAPTER 7

The Master's Great Refinery

Everyone waited patiently for his or her assignment after the white-robed assistant finished speaking. Hungry Heart imagined the beautiful gold and silver paradigm pieces that she was certain the Master would ask her to inspect or, at the very least, polish. Such a job would surely take place far away from the heat and sweat of the fire. Although she did feel better about being at the refinery, she still could not bring herself to look down toward the burning core. How could anyone go down there? Immersed in her own thoughts, she never noticed Sacrificial Heart moving from one person to another with quiet words of assurance before disappearing from Hungry Heart's view.

"Hungry hearts, all hungry hearts, over here, please," the announcement sounded. "All joyful hearts to the left, pious hearts to the right, and grateful hearts down there…"

One by one, hearts of every description moved to their designated areas. Hungry Heart's group buzzed with excitement until an assistant approached. His words stunned everyone.

"Hungry hearts, the Master would like you to feed the fire."

"Feed the fire? Who…us? There must be some mistake," a pretentious hungry heart declared firmly.

"No one can go down there. It's impossible!" Hungry Heart protested. "It's much too dangerous for even the strongest hearts!"

Their pleas failed to dissuade the assistant from his mission.

"There is no mistake. The fire must be fed continually so that it burns evenly. The searching hearts will bring in the dead wood from the mountain, and you will feed the fire. It is very important not to let the fire go out.

It must burn day and night. This is an awesome responsibility; the Master depends upon your faithful service. See, they have already started collecting the wood for you."

Speechless, the group of disappointed hungry hearts watched him move on to the next section of travelers. Seconds barely passed before the grumbling started.

"Why didn't he choose the worker hearts to feed the fire? They love hard work, and besides, they're much better suited for it. Why, we are students of life and seekers of truth, not manual laborers!"

Hungry Heart mumbled under her breath with the rest. Her eyes scanned the area for a way of escape. Just then she heard the Master's voice calling to her from far away.

"Hungry Heart, feed my fire. I want to teach you about the hunger that burns in your own heart."

Without another word, she left the disgruntled hungry hearts and started toward a narrow path that led down to the burning center. The wind picked up as she descended, and the smoke made it difficult to see very far ahead. Hungry Heart stumbled down the smoke-filled walkway until she reached a circular stone stairway. This led up to a walled edge, which held back the hungry flames. The enormous stone wall stood around the flaming crater, creating a gigantic open-air furnace. The heat was almost unbearable. *I shall die in this place. I shall surely die,* her heart cried. *This can't be happening. I must have been tricked and am in the Land of the Lost surrounded by spirit creatures!*

No sooner had those thoughts flashed through her mind than, with a strange sense of fearful awe, she felt the Master's presence. The assistant's words came back to her. *The Master actually walked out of the catacombs with his eyes ablaze! He proclaimed everyone's debts to be paid in full and declared free citizenship for all. It is said that he sits on a throne of fire on the Third Mountain to remind his enemies that he will live forever!*

With a strange sense of peace, Hungry Heart silently dedicated herself to the Master's service. *Master, I will feed this fire because it belongs to you. You have been here ahead of me. I am not afraid.*

With a start, she opened her eyes at a touch on her elbow. An assistant motioned for her to follow him to one of the many small openings in the refinery wall. To the left of this opening, which was about the size of her grandfather's oven door, an assortment of shovels and fire tongs hung from large hooks. To the right lay several empty wood bins.

The searching hearts returned from the deep woods with huge pieces of dead wood and dragged them down to the bins at Hungry Heart's workstation. Hour after hour she labored, pushing heavy dead tree limbs through the opening. Sometimes she asked for help with the larger pieces, but most of the time she managed alone. After she found an old ax among the tools hanging on the wall, she chopped the big limbs into manageable pieces. Though her back ached and blisters appeared on her hands, she kept working. Sometimes sparks from the fire jumped through the opening and singed her clothes. However, the more difficult it became, the more determinedly she worked. Oddly enough, the fire did not burn or harm her body in any way.

"Hungry Heart, would you like a drink of cool water?"

The voice sounded like that of an angel, and she turned around to see a religious heart holding a small cup in her hands. Religious hearts were known for their knowledge of the Great Book and for their wonderful teaching ability. Many people aspired to become religious hearts because such hearts spent all their time thinking about the wonderful ways of the Master and extolling his greatness. One hardly, if ever, found a religious heart serving water to dirty workers. But then, who ever expected to find a hungry heart working at a hot and dirty fire?

Hungry Heart accepted the water and smiled, too tired to ask the religious heart any questions. After swallowing the last drop of precious liquid, she returned to her station, throwing branches, logs, pieces of lumber, leaves, and anything that burned into the fire. Regardless of what she fed the fire, it always demanded more.

As the first day drew to a close, someone led her out to the workers' living quarters and gave her supper while another hungry heart took her place to keep feeding the fire. She accepted the small meal, ate it, and lay down on her cot. *I'll just lie down for a few minutes, and then I must find Sacrificial Heart*, she mused, but within moments her weary body yielded to much-needed sleep.

The next morning, Hungry Heart started looking for Sacrificial Heart. It was time to move on and continue their journey. She was in for a rude awakening.

"Hungry Heart, what are you doing here in the casting area?" an assistant found her and asked.

"I'm looking for Sacrificial Heart, my companion. It's time to move on in our journey," she replied.

"It is not time yet. There is still more work to be done," the assistant said as he guided Hungry Heart back to her workstation. She was too surprised to protest.

The next day Hungry Heart went back to feed the fire—and the next, and the next, and the next. Eventually Hungry Heart lost track of time. She could not remember when she had seen Sacrificial Heart last, and sometimes she even questioned her own love for the Master.

Each day proved to be more difficult than the last. The fire never harmed her, but bruises covered her body and her back ached from the hard labor.

She cried to the Master, "What more must I do to prove my love for you? What do you want?"

Although he did not make his presence known, she could hear his voice coming from the flames. His answer never changed.

"Feed my fire, Hungry Heart, feed my fire. My fire must never die."

Every time he spoke, she managed to keep going a little while longer; and every time one of the assistants announced, "You are free to leave whenever you choose," she decided to stay.

One evening, during a rare discussion with a fellow hungry heart, she admitted, "It's strange, isn't it? I am free to leave, yet I am a prisoner. Where would I go? I know that I can't go back. As difficult as this is, I do not want to return to a life of endless searching for a place of appointment in the Master's service. I can't go ahead to continue my journey because I do not know where to go. At least here I know that I am doing what he is asking me to do."

The very next morning the searching hearts did not return from the deep woods with the usual supply of fuel. Hungry Heart watched the fire anxiously as it burned lower and lower. She gathered up every last fragment that she could find from the wood bins and threw them in. Others noticed the diminishing flames as well.

Someone cried out loudly, "The fire is dying! The Master wants it to burn day and night. It must never go out!"

A deep sense of failure swept over Hungry Heart. After all this time and the endless hours of painful labor, the fire was dying right in front of their eyes.

In desperation she cried out, "Master, the fire is dying! We have no more wood! What shall we do?"

Again, the Master's voice seemed to emanate from the fire itself, "What do you have that you do not need?"

"What do I have that I do not need? Master, you don't understand, the fire is dying! The searching hearts have not come with wood..." her voice cracked in a high-pitched plea.

"Feed my fire, Hungry Heart."

Hungry Heart looked around in desperation. Her eyes caught a glimpse of something lying in the corner. It was her small overnight satchel leaning against a wood bin. Although she had insisted on bringing her diary and precious books, she had had no time to write or read. The small mementos from home had not brought her the comfort she expected. The clothes were impractical for the work, and the Master provided everything she needed from day to day. She stared at the dying fire through the opening at her workstation and made her decision. With a quick motion she grabbed the bag and threw it into the fire.

The hungry flames leaped into the air and cracked at her sacrifice. But rather than falling back and diminishing once again, they burned bigger and brighter than ever before! The heat, almost unbearable before, now started to feel like warm sunshine on a spring day. A gust of wind picked up the smoke and carried it up to the heavens. Suddenly, Hungry Heart could see everything around her clearly, including what she needed to do!

"Hurry, everyone! Throw the things that you do not need into the fire. We must keep the Master's fire burning! Hurry! Those things are of no use to us here. The Master gives us everything we need. He is our provider. If we insist on keeping them, his fire will die!"

People came from everywhere and tossed needless personal belongings into the fire. It burned and burned and burned. Hungry Heart stood back and watched the scene unfold around her. Their sacrificial love for the Master far exceeded all the days and nights of labor. Everything the Master needed for his fire lay at their own feet.

A wonderful sense of peace settled over the refinery. For the first time since her arrival, Hungry Heart felt the hunger within her own heart subside. Now she understood that the Master did not need her hours of painful labor and self-reliance, which only made his fire hungrier. Instead, he needed the dead wood of her own life, the things she no longer needed.

In understanding the Master's request, Hungry Heart gained understanding of herself. Her relentless search for knowledge only made her heart hungrier. It mattered little how many meetings she traveled to or how many teachers she heard. Like feeding the fire, the harder she worked to satisfy her hunger, the more difficult it became to satisfy. Although she did not understand exactly what or why, she knew that there were certain things in her life she did not need any longer. When she let go of these things, she would receive over and above her deepest need.

That night, as Hungry Heart lay down under the stars, she thanked the Master for allowing her to come to this wonderful, wonderful place.

CHAPTER 8

Sacrificial Heart's Paradigm

The refinery fire burned brightly as hungry hearts relinquished the things they no longer needed. Searching hearts returned from the mountains dancing and singing while pious hearts discovered that only the Master's love could make their lives shine like polished gold. Religious hearts learned creative new ways to express their knowledge of the Master; others, for the very first time, actually heard the sound of his voice and acknowledged his great sacrificial love.

Each one received a paradigm piece to symbolize the new truth in his or her life. The Master himself arrived at the presentation ceremony. He was dressed in a plain white linen robe that looked much like the ones worn by his assistants. His, however, sparkled in the sunlight.

Hungry Heart whispered in Sacrificial Heart's ear, "I have never seen him looking so radiant or so happy, have you?"

Sacrificial Heart gently touched her shoulder with one hand and pointed to the dancing flames in the burning volcanic core with the other.

"His joy is complete because he knows that the fire of his love has touched our hearts. Look over there at the refinery fire. See how brightly it burns today? Yet, as bright as it is, it is only a shadow compared to the fire that burns in his heart for us. Hush now, he's coming."

Hungry Heart watched in awe as the Master approached Sacrificial Heart. She lifted her head for him to gaze intently into her eyes. Without a word spoken between them, she lowered her head and nodded in agreement. The Master smiled, touched his finger to her chin and lifted her head to meet his gaze again. His other hand reached out and placed something in her hand. As she closed her eyes and fell to her knees weeping, he turned and approached Hungry Heart with a hearty laugh.

"Hungry Heart! Just look at you! You are no longer a child, you are a young woman! Get ready, I have some surprises waiting for you on this journey."

A few moments earlier, Hungry Heart had been filled with dozens of questions, but in his presence she forgot each and every one. The sound of his laughter filled her heart with a sense of unspeakable joy until she found herself standing there, in the midst of this solemn occasion, laughing with him.

It's difficult to tell how long they stood there laughing together like old friends, but eventually they both quieted down. As Hungry Heart paused to catch her breath, the Master placed the long-awaited paradigm piece in her hand with a tender word.

"Always keep my love burning in your heart. Allow it to burn up the things you do not need, and I will give you everything you do need."

Hungry Heart rubbed her fingers over the tiny item in her hand—a small golden flame with sparkling red rubies. It was, by far, the most beautiful of all her pieces. By the time she stopped admiring it and looked up to thank him, he had moved on to the next one in line.

After the ceremony, everyone had an opportunity to exclaim over one another's new pieces and to visit other sections of the refinery. They saw how the raw metals were processed, purified to perfection and then molded into gold and silver symbols, which were later embedded with beautiful gemstones from the mountain mines.

After each paradigm piece was created, the Master's assistants carefully documented it according to its point of reference in the Great Book and the individual receiving it. After documentation, couriers immediately carried it to the Master, and he bestowed it to the designated heart. Although the truth itself always remained the same, the reflection of truth varied from one individual to another. Hungry Heart marveled at the Master's refining process and appreciated her collection even more than ever. Her paradigm was indeed a precious gift from the Master, designed specifically for her alone.

"It's time to go, Hungry Heart," Sacrificial Heart nudged her.

"Must we?"

"You are free to stay here if you like, but you are ready to continue your journey now. The choice, as always, is yours."

Hungry Heart placed the golden flame in the blue bag she carried over her heart and followed Sacrificial Heart with a sense of regret as well as anticipation. She had learned so much here about life, about herself and above all, about the Master's love. Up until now she had been preoccupied with her own journey, but remembering Sacrificial Heart's encounter with the Master she asked, "Sacrificial Heart, you love the Master very much, don't you?"

"Yes, I do. However, he loves all of us so much more than we will ever be able to love him in return."

She lifted her right hand just enough for Hungry Heart to see the small gold ring on her finger.

"Oh, Sacrificial Heart, you have received your paradigm! It is beautiful...and so perfect!"

One tiny broken heart, no bigger than a barley seed, lay embedded in a larger heart. Despite its simplicity, the little ring was magnificent. Paradigm rings were not common. They signified a special bond between the recipient and the Master, one that usually meant forsaking everything and everyone. Hungry Heart pleaded earnestly, "Please tell me the story."

Two curious hearts dashed over at the sound of her voice, so Sacrificial Heart wisely suggested, "Let's be on our way. I'll tell you while we travel."

Curious hearts were sometimes known for having a less-than-sincere curiosity in paradigm stories. They tended to lose interest quickly as soon as something more fascinating presented itself. However, she graciously included them and spoke loudly enough for everyone to hear as they walked away from the refinery grounds.

"Before I came to the Master's refinery I took great pride in my sacrificial heart. I gave everything that I owned away and sacrificed my life in every way possible for the Master. People knew that I could be counted on to always put others before myself and to give myself to any worthy cause in the kingdom of Christianity. During my first visit to the refinery, all the sacrificial hearts were assigned the duty of skimming the impurities from the vats of liquid gold. It was a most sacrificial task, and I was quite pleased with my duties.

"One day the Master stopped by. I was all covered with soot and sweat from spending hours over the hot vats. I expected him to be quite pleased with my sacrifice, but he didn't even notice. He only seemed to care about the granules floating on the surface of the molten gold. My heart sank, but I convinced myself to work harder for his approval. After that, he came by every day to look at the liquid gold, but never at me. Attempting to sacrifice more, I even gave away my meals on occasion, and he still refused to notice."

Hungry Heart listened intently. She could not imagine the Master deliberately ignoring Sacrificial Heart's labor of love. After all, sacrificial service ranked high among Christianity's basic expectations, something that Hungry Heart had often admired in others but had never been very good at.

No, Hungry Heart usually ended up watching someone else do whatever needed to be done, just as she had watched Loving Heart serve her guests in Grandfather's kitchen. Her parents and grandparents often sacrificed their own desires for someone else's needs. Why, Grandmother Trusting Heart had given herself to every needy heart in town. Some said that's why the Master took her to his heavens at such an early age—she just gave and gave until she had no more left to give. In fact, Hungry Heart had always been surrounded by hearts who needed to give. *Maybe,* she reasoned to herself, *that is why it was so difficult for me to give the Master the things in my life that I did not need. I just never learned how to give myself away—even to the Master himself.*

However, here was Sacrificial Heart, giving her own food away to please him, and he had not responded with approval. *How strange, how very strange this sounded. Why was he more concerned about his gold than her heart?* The temptation to dismiss Sacrificial Heart's story rose up.

After all, the elders had taught her so many times, "If it doesn't agree with our teachings from the meeting place, disregard it. Do not be led astray by strange and diverse ideas, for they only will lead to your destruction. People from the border countries try to slip in with counterfeit paradigms from time to time. You must learn to always be on guard."

But Hungry Heart knew Sacrificial Heart and her love for the Master. She had watched them together. No, there was something more here—something more than she had learned from the meeting places and the elders who encouraged everyone to work as hard as possible for the Master's approval. Sacrificial Heart continued to speak with a faraway look in her eyes, as if she was someplace else.

"I grew very discouraged, but I never let him see it. I even asked others to warn me when they saw him coming so that I might appear strong for him. This is what my parents and elders had taught me to do. I labored hard for many months, watching others receive their paradigms and move on to the Second Mountain, but I had to remain. One day the Master came by and caught me in a dreadful state. It broke my heart to have him find me weak and brokenhearted. I fell on my knees and begged him to forgive me and to give me another chance. I'll never forget his words.

"'Sacrificial Heart, I do not want your sacrifices of labor. I want your broken heart. I want the impurities, the pride and self-seeking, so that I can refine you as gold.'

"He pointed to the impurities floating on the molten surface. 'This is what I am doing in your life. I am refining you. Now, will you give me your broken heart so that I can give you a new one?' "

At this point, the two curious hearts left to follow a larger crowd gathered off to the left, but Sacrificial Heart did not seem to notice or care. Her voice grew stronger, and she spoke with unwavering love for the Master.

"He changed my heart that day. Oh, I still give willingly of my possessions and my time, but I do not give them to gain the Master's approval. He wants me to offer the imperfections, the brokenness, and the inadequacies that surface in my life day by day. As I give him my broken heart, he changes me. My concerns are so small and insignificant compared to his great love for everyone. We are only seeds, and we need to be planted firmly in the great seedbed of his heart. Today he looked into my heart and asked me to stay here on the First Mountain. I have agreed to serve him here."

Hungry Heart watched the sunlight pour through the evergreen trees in front of them. In the far distance she could see the mountaintop of the Second Mountain, and her heart yearned for distant places. Sacrificial Heart might never travel there or experience the glory of the Master's Third Dwelling. *What a tremendous sacrifice, to be willing to stay here on the First Mountain,* she thought to herself. *Surely, it's a good place, but can it possibly compare to what lies ahead?*

Sacrificial Heart could almost hear her friend's thoughts. She lovingly rescued her from the awkward moment.

"I know, Hungry Heart. I once longed to make the journey to the Third Mountain also. I planned to endure the hardships with great sacrificial love. Yet, now I know that the greatest sacrifice I can give to the Master is to stay here in my place of appointment. Remember, it isn't how far we go that is important."

"I know, it's why we are going that makes the difference. But you wanted to go because you love the Master, so how can that be wrong?"

"Because I wanted his approval more than I wanted him, and that desire had become an impurity in my heart. If I stay here and serve him on the First Mountain, I stay because I want to be with him, nothing more."

"Nothing more?"

"Nothing."

"Not even to go home to tell others where you are and what you are doing?"

"Not even that. I have sent word with the Master's messengers. It is enough. I do not need to be congratulated for great sacrifices any longer. My heart belongs to the Master." Sacrificial Heart paused. "Enough about this for now. Sometimes it is better to allow truth to grow instead of trying to pick it. Come on, I think you are going to be surprised with the rest of the First Mountain!"

CHAPTER 9

The Lagoon of Truth

As the travelers descended the mountain of the Great Refinery, a beautiful vista opened up in front of them. Before them two great cascading waterfalls emptied into a mountainside lagoon that fed into the Great Ocean to the north. The outermost eastern mountain slopes embraced the pool, and smooth rock-terraced steps led down to the water. A group of happy hearts brushed past them with cheers of delight as Hungry Heart paused in awe.

"What is this place? I have never seen anything so peaceful or so perfect..."

Her voice trailed off, searching for words to describe the unforgettable scene in front of her. Bushy-tailed squirrels chased each other playfully in and out of the trees while small yellow birds sang. Tree limbs weighed down with heavy white blossoms bowed low, lightly kissing the water's surface. Several tall, graceful deer stood statuesquely against a thick grove of soft-needled pine trees, unafraid of the travelers and the Master's assistants. If perfection could be found anywhere, it was here. Men, animals, and nature moved in complete harmony.

Pointing to the crystal clear water sparkling under the afternoon sun, Sacrificial Heart explained, "This is the Master's Lagoon of Truth. At the refinery, his truth is forged in the fire. Here, his truth refreshes us, cleanses us, and quenches our thirst. Speaking of thirst, I'll bet you are just as thirsty as I am. Get ready, I'll race you to the water!"

The lighthearted challenge took Hungry Heart by surprise, but within moments the two women were darting down the terraced steps to the water's edge where they knelt down and scooped up handfuls of clear water.

Laughing, Hungry Heart bent over to splash some water at Sacrificial Heart. Then she caught a glimpse of her reflection in the water. *Oh no!* she thought. *I look terrible!* Refinery soot still covered her clothing, and her tangled hair needed attention quite badly. Shamefully, she remembered meeting the Master in such a state.

Her appearance did not seem to disturb Sacrificial Heart, who waded into the water to wash. Hungry Heart gladly followed her. The water, which moments ago felt so wonderfully cool to her parched lips, now enveloped her tired body like a warm bath. They slipped beneath the surface to rinse the soot from their hair and laughed and splashed like little girls on a summer swim. Other travelers joined them until the entire lagoon echoed with joy and laughter. The memory of long hours of refinery labor receded far behind them.

When the two young women finally waded back to shore, they found clean, soft white linen garments waiting for them on the grass. The nearby trees and bushes provided them privacy to change, and several helpful hearts built a campfire by the lagoon so they could dry their hair. The entire group ended the day exchanging stories about the Master's love over a picnic supper. A few hours later, warm, fed, and blissfully tired, Hungry Heart followed an assistant, who directed them to small tents with soft mats and pillows.

"What a wonderful day," she sighed in contentment as her head hit the pillow.

The next morning came all too swiftly. Hungry Heart abruptly woke out of a sweet sleep when Sacrificial Heart nudged her playfully.

"Wake up, sleepy head! It's time to wash in the Master's pool!"

Puzzled, Hungry Heart rubbed her eyes and then shut them again, almost forgetting where she was.

"Hungry Heart, wake up!"

Still a bit groggy from sleep, Hungry Heart climbed from the tent and followed Sacrificial Heart to the water's edge. She stared at her reflection in the pool and rubbed her eyes yet again. *How could that be?* Her hands and feet were dirty once more, and her new white garments looked as if she had been working all night instead of sleeping. *Curious,* she thought to herself. *How did this happen?* Obediently, she followed Sacrificial Heart's lead and washed as before.

Within a few minutes they stepped from the water sparkling clean again and joined the others for roasted grains and fruit. After breakfast, one of the Master's assistants climbed the terraced steps overlooking the lagoon until he was high enough to be seen by everyone.

"Welcome to the Master's Lagoon of Truth. These waters will refresh you, and we are here to serve you. There are no schedules to keep or duties to perform. You are free to mingle with each other, join in serious discussions, engage in lighthearted play or just rest. Take this opportunity to share your new paradigm pieces and consider the lessons you learned at the refinery. We always will be close at hand to answer your questions and to help in any way possible.

"There is only one thing we ask of you—please keep clean. You will not be permitted to enter the Master's Dwelling Place on the Second Mountain until you have clean hands and a pure heart. The waters are here for you, so please go to them for frequent and thorough washings. Again, if you have any questions, do not hesitate to ask. Enjoy your time of refreshing, one and all."

At first Hungry Heart marveled at the apparent lack of regiment. However, by midday, the complexity of simplicity set in. Her morning conversation with a group of curious hearts left her looking as though she had been making mud pies. She found Sacrificial Heart kneeling at the pool washing a few smudges from her own hands and arms and did not waste any time expressing her indignation.

"Look at me, just look at me! I can't imagine how I got this dirty. You know, this place looks clean, but I think the Master should get someone to clean off those benches over there. They must be filthy. The last group through here must have been very careless. Just look at me!"

Sacrificial Heart ignored this outburst. Instead she simply smiled, finished washing her hands, and stood up. "Why don't you wash before we eat? You will feel much better."

A bit miffed with her friend's apparent disinterest, Hungry Heart stepped into the warm waters, took a deep breath and dipped her head beneath the water's surface. As before, she stepped from the waters sparkling clean and refreshed. Even her attitude changed. Instead of complaining about the dirty benches and Sacrificial Heart's lack of agreement, she started to sing a little tune, found a bucket, and washed them off herself.

The midday meal consisted of milk and delicious fresh warm bread. One of the Master's assistants spoke to the group while they ate.

"The Master's truth washes our hearts. A clean heart is very important to the Master because a clean heart has room for love, compassion, and enlightenment. Here at the Master's Lagoon of Truth, your outward appearance is only a reflection of your innermost heart."

Hungry Heart smoothed a tiny wrinkle from her still-clean white garment and nodded in agreement. Indeed, she felt loving and compassionate, even a bit enlightened today. Like everyone else, she wanted her heart to be sparkling clean.

As time wore on, Hungry Heart noticed that Sacrificial Heart seemed to be spending less and less time with her, but she dismissed the temptation to feel left out. Instead Hungry Heart joined her new friends under the white blossomed trees during the afternoon. It felt so good to laugh again. Besides, it gave her the perfect opportunity to tell the others about the Master's hearty laughter at the refinery.

One serious heart, a tall young man with eloquent speech, took exception to her account.

"Do you think that laughter is proper behavior for the Master? After all, he is a king and should maintain his dignity, don't you think? I've heard about elders who actually encourage laughter in their meeting places. No, no, I'm not certain that you actually heard the Master laugh. I think that you mistook laughter for his joy."

"But," questioned Hungry Heart, "what is the difference between laughter and joy?"

"Oh, there is a big difference. Laughter is disrespectful, you know, and sometimes very loud. It is always emotional, and we must guard against too much emotion. Joy is sweet, always very sweet."

"But I know I heard him laugh, and he made me laugh."

"No, no. You must not tell people that, or you shall create all manner of confusion."

On and on Hungry Heart debated the issue with her new friend, Serious Heart, until she started to doubt her experience at the refinery. Once Serious Heart instilled enough questions for serious thought, he ended the discussion with, "Of course, we all have to examine our perception of truth from time to time. I am certain you will be able to see things more clearly now."

Hungry Heart offered him a weak smile and left to find one of the Master's assistants. She needed to talk to someone—and where was Sacrificial Heart?

Soon Hungry Heart found an assistant sitting alone underneath a white grapevine arbor a few yards from the water, reading the Great Book. He smiled as she approached and invited her to sit down. Hesitantly at first, but gaining confidence with each word, she explained her dilemma, finishing with, "What do you think? Does the Master laugh? How could Serious Heart possibly say such things? Who does he think he is? I know what I heard..."

"Whether the Master laughs or not is not what I am concerned most about right now. Hungry Heart, look at you," he motioned her to the edge of the pool. "Go ahead, look at your reflection in the pool. First you need to wash. Then come back, and we will talk."

Poor Hungry Heart! She faced her soiled reflection one more time before she glanced back over her shoulder to see the assistant still waving his hand at her and motioning her forward. Slowly and remorsefully, she stepped into the water. Why did this keep happening to her? She could not stay clean for more than a couple of hours at a time.

An hour or so later, clean and dry, she returned to the assistant.

"I don't understand. I just don't understand all this, but I want to. Please help me to learn what it means to have clean hands and a pure heart so that I can go on to the Second Mountain."

"Let's look at what has been happening," the assistant began. "Do you see any pattern?"

"Well," Hungry Heart said thoughtfully, "I wash in the pool and come out clean. Then I try to stay clean, but I always end up just as filthy as before."

"What are you doing between washings?"

"Eating, talking to others, playing, just...well...it just seems impossible to live here without becoming dirty! Everything looks clean, but I keep getting messy."

"That is true in part. Wherever you go, whatever you do, you come in contact with unclean things, thoughts, and ideas, despite your best intentions. However, it isn't these things that defile your heart, it is your reaction to them. Serious Heart could have used more wisdom in his conversation; however, it was your reaction to him that defiled your heart, not his words. Think about it. Now that you have washed in the Lagoon of Truth, how should you have reacted?"

Hungry Heart lowered her head humbly. "Like the Master himself, with understanding and compassion. Serious Heart's inability to understand my experience did not measure the truth of the matter; it only measured my desire to be right."

"Well spoken, Hungry Heart. This is why the Master has provided his truth for you, and this is why it is so important for you to learn to wash in it. When your heart is clean, your response to the people and the things around you will be clean. Then you will be a fit servant in the Master's Dwelling Place."

"Will I always have to return to the waters several times a day? If I do, how will I ever be able to continue my journey?"

Smiling, he pointed to several people swimming beyond the lagoon in the Great Ocean. "Until you learn to swim like a fish in the deep waters of the Master's truth, you will always need to come back and wash. But knowing you, Hungry Heart, I don't think it will take you very long."

The assistant closed the Great Book, stood to his feet, patted her on the shoulder, and left her alone with her thoughts. Swim like a fish—whatever did he mean? Still feeling crisp and clean, an overwhelming sense of love for the Master filled her heart.

She ran to the water's edge and cried out, "Master, teach me to swim in the deep waters of your truth."

Without another thought, she arched her body and dove into the sun-lit waters. Deeper and deeper she went until her lungs felt like bursting. Only then did she rise to the surface for air. One deep breath filled her with new confidence and strength, and she swam still farther from the shore. Everything seemed so clear in the waters of his truth, so effortless, so clean, and so pure. People, faces, situations, arguments, debates, habits, and decisions flashed before her mind's eye like the rolling waters in front of her. She swam through the water with the boldness of an agile sea creature because she now saw the seas of her life through the clear waters of the Master's truth.

It is impossible to tell how long she swam or how far out she ventured because, as she learned so long ago at the first gate, time in the Master's Dwelling Place is not measured by human limitations. Everything that ever was and ever will be happens all at once. He lives in the past, present, and future. Someplace, at sometime, immersed in His truth, she decided to return to shore and tell everyone what she had learned.

Swimming out had been effortless, but surprisingly, going back proved to be very difficult. The shifting waves pulled her away from the security of the barely visible shoreline. Every time she struggled to swim on her own, the current resisted her efforts. She called out for the Master's help or for anyone nearby to come to her aid, but help did not come. The waters of truth simply refused to allow her to chart her own course for land.

"Master! What is happening? Have I come here to die?"

Finally, exhausted, she yielded to the deep waters and cried out one last time, "Master!"

Helpless, her body sank below the sun-lit waters into the dark depths of eternal truth. There, in the abyss of her own unconscious, the Master's truth flowed in and out of her as freely as the air itself. Her own humanity yielded and adapted to the Master's miraculous waters. When Hungry Heart regained consciousness later, she found herself instinctively swimming with the grace and strength of a dolphin. For hours, days, or perhaps even weeks in ordinary time, she swam through the waters of truth, on the surface and beneath, with others and alone.

Finally, she heard the Master's voice in the wind.

"Hungry Heart, it's time to go back now. Go—the winds will carry you home."

This time the currents carried her effortlessly back to land. Sacrificial Heart stood on the shore and greeted her with a tender smile.

"It's good to have you back, Hungry Heart. You look wonderful."

"I'm not sure what happened out there in the water, or how long I have been gone..." Hungry Heart's voice trailed off in a sense of bewilderment. She searched for words to describe her experience when Sacrificial Heart rescued her with understanding assurance.

"You learned to swim in the waters of the Master's truth. From now on, it will be within you wherever you go. The deep waters always will be inside you, but it will be up to you to appropriate them wisely." She added, "You'll see and understand what this means in the days ahead. As for time, it does not matter. His truth is eternal. Besides, the time is perfect because now you are ready to travel to the Second Mountain!"

"The Second Mountain?" exclaimed Hungry Heart. "Are you sure? When do we start?"

"Yes, I'm sure. You'll leave just as soon as the others are assembled, but I will not be going," Sacrificial Heart said. "Remember, my place of appointment is here on the First Mountain. Besides, you no longer need me.

The Master's truth will guide you from here. The impurities in our hearts often prevent us from seeing him, but you have learned to swim in his truth now, so you will be able to keep your eyes on him for the rest of your journey."

Hungry Heart understood, and she embraced her companion. The two promised to send greetings with the mountain messengers from time to time. Although Hungry Heart was sorry to leave her friend, she had to continue her paradigm quest. Sacrificial Heart knew her place and purpose in the Master's service; her paradigm was complete. Hungry Heart's life still lay in fragmented pieces in the little blue bag over her heart. She had no choice but to journey on.

When Hungry Heart turned away, she saw a figure nearby. The Master himself stood waiting for her just a few feet away! As she ran toward him, he held out something shining in his hand. He smiled, placed a small silver dolphin in her hand and motioned for her to follow him.

PART THREE

THE

Second Mountain

CHAPTER 10

The Golden Gateway

———•◦•———

The Master led Hungry Heart down the steep descent from one mountain to the next. Dark green rock moss, which drank moisture from underground springs, hugged the shaded mountainside. Clusters of tiny white galax, nested amongst shiny round dark green leaves, greeted the sunbeams. Sometimes the obscure trail led through dense vine-covered underbrush, heavy with the scent of honeysuckle, but the Master knew the way and considerately cleared a path for Hungry Heart to follow him. He seemed to love the mysterious dark coves as much as the open trails.

Every day, the misty morning fog always lifted and invited the rising sun to penetrate the deepest ravines. At day's end, the northern lights in the sky danced like heavenly candles appointed to keep watch through the night. As long as Hungry Heart rested in the "now moment" and kept her eyes on the Master, her heart danced with joy in his company.

If she failed to stay focused, dangers and distractions besieged her. Once she lingered at a turn on the path and gazed hopefully toward the Second Mountain. Myriads of mountain streams and waterfalls reflected the sunlight until the entire mountain shimmered with a golden glow. Breathless with excitement, her long-forgotten urges returned.

The Second Mountain! Oh, how I wish I could fly like a bird and soar to the mountaintops right now! I wonder how long it will take me to get there and what the Master will ask me to do when I arrive? Surely there must be a faster way to get there than this path. She laughed to herself. Wistfully she thought, *I have learned so much, surely I can learn to fly! The Master can travel anywhere in a moment of time; I wonder why this journey is taking so long?*

Lost in her own fantasies, Hungry Heart's foot hit a loose rock. Knocked off balance, she landed partway over the edge of the narrow trail.

"Whoa there, Hungry Heart. You don't want to get to the bottom of this mountain that fast, do you?" The Master's strong hand grabbed her arm and pulled her back to the path.

Embarrassed and quite shaken, she inched away from the dangerous edge. She could have tumbled down the embankment onto the sharp rocks below and been painfully wounded, if not killed.

"Oh, Master, thank you. I just took my eyes from the path for a moment. The beauty of the Second Mountain distracted me. Besides, this path is very steep and the stones are so loose. The sunlight was so bright, I could not see you clearly, and the wind blew in my eyes," Hungry Heart stuttered on with one excuse after another.

The Master's face slowly clouded with disappointment. Clearly unable to justify herself, Hungry Heart finally grew silent and waited for his response. His dark warm eyes ignored every one of her arguments as he gently addressed the distractions in her heart.

"Right now, your attention should be here, on this path, and your eyes on me. Careful steps will take you where you need to go to see everything you need to see. You must learn to place your hope in me, not in where you are going or what you will do when you get there. Distraction will make your feet wander from the path in front of you. But I think you have just learned that."

Hungry Heart hung her head. She allowed him to dust her off and attend to her bruises. As he did so, he reminded her kindly, "Keep your eyes on me, Hungry Heart. I go before you to make certain that your path is safe."

Warm dark eyes pierced her heart. The firm, unconditional love radiating from his voice conveyed both chastisement and comfort. Within moments they were laughing again, and she promised to stop daydreaming. The rest of the day she thought about the Master's words. She watched him carefully as she sang little tunes from the meeting places and waved to fellow travelers going up and down the mountainside on nearby trails.

Their presence did not surprise Hungry Heart. Everyone in the kingdom of Christianity knew that the Master could be in many places at the same time, comforting some, leading others, and meeting just about every need imaginable. Exactly how he did this remained a mystery, but then almost everything about the Master was a mystery until he imparted paradigm pieces of truth. It only took a glance in the others' directions to know that they, too, followed the Master on a path specifically suited for their lives.

Without warning, a group of cautious hearts jumped between her and the Master, waving their arms frantically. She braced herself and stepped back. Cautious hearts were good-hearted, even though they suffered from poor eyesight and simply did not believe anything or anyone beyond what their dim eyes could see. Coming from the Plains of Hope, Hungry Heart lived with hope for the unseen; thus, she often found herself at odds with cautious hearts.

"Stop! Stop! Do not go any further! You must not leave the First Mountain! Go back to the Lagoon of Truth where it is safe," one cautious heart cried in her face.

She greeted him politely, deliberately stepped around him, then remarked, "Don't worry, I know where I am going. The Master is just ahead, and I am following him to the Second Mountain."

"No! No! No! You must not go there. We have heard such terrible stories about life there. Why, sometimes we can even hear the cries from across the valley. Just yesterday we had to help a traveler find his way back to the lagoon. He, just like you, expected the Second Mountain to be a wonderful place. Not true! They robbed him and left him to die just after he passed through the gate. He, too, tried to follow the Master. Please Hungry Heart, listen to us."

Their words stopped her like a lasso around her neck. She spun around on one heel and faced the curious hearts.

"Who robbed him? What are you talking about?"

When they saw that they had her full attention, the cautious hearts all began to clamor at once.

"Yes! The relentless hearts beat him. They pounded him so badly that he could not stand up. He only wanted to pass through, but they were determined to make him one of them. They pulled him this way and that way until the poor thing almost died."

"Ohhh," Hungry Heart gasped. She knew cautious hearts sometimes exaggerated; still, they did not lie. "Why should anyone do such a thing?"

"Oh, the Second Mountain is a fearful place," one short, chubby cautious heart exclaimed fearfully.

"Yes, it is a fearful place indeed," another one agreed. "It belongs to the Master, but years ago the travelers set up camps all over the mountain. Now they defend their territory and do everything they can to entice unsuspecting people like you to join them. If you refuse, the most dreadful things will happen."

"Oh yes, the most dreadful things," the rest all chorused.

Hungry Heart rejected their wild tales courteously. They sounded too much like those she had heard at Grandfather's house after the North Wind had blown through.

"Surely you must be mistaken. The Master never allows such things to take place."

"He does! He does!" squealed a little cautious heart from the back of the group. "Look, look over there, see for yourself if you don't believe us!"

Her eyes followed his waving hand to see several people limping in her direction. They were so bruised and broken that it was impossible to hear anything from their hearts except despair. They stopped briefly to warn her about the hard taskmasters they had just encountered on the Second Mountain, and told her how some freedom hearts had helped them to escape.

"Now," one woman cried softly, "we are going back to the Valley of Despair. We are too broken to swim in the lagoon and too weak to serve at the refinery. The Master has promised to meet us there and to bind our wounds with his love. If you go, be careful. Remember to keep your eyes on the Master."

The wounded hearts moved on before she could respond, and the cautious hearts started flagging down the travelers coming behind her. Taskmasters? Robbers? Rebel groups? On the Second Mountain? Perhaps the cautious hearts were right. Perhaps I should be content to stay at the lagoon. This journey is dangerous; I did almost fall off the cliff.

The entire encounter so unsettled her that she lost sight of the Master. Evidently he had kept moving when she stopped to listen to the curious hearts. Unable to see him any longer, she sat down on an old log and reconsidered her journey.

I've already received two very precious new paradigm pieces. Maybe I should be satisfied. Carefully, she pulled the blue bag from over her heart and poured her pieces out on her lap.

Although a few pieces seemed to fit together, many more were still missing. *Maybe the Master wants me to stay on the First Mountain like Sacrificial Heart? Is this what he was trying to tell me when I slipped? Maybe I should go back to the Valley of Despair to serve the Master with my parents and Grandfather Humble Heart. Or Cousin Mercy Heart, or Loving Heart.* She contemplated one option after another. Confused, she closed her eyes for a moment. When she opened them, the Master stood waiting just ahead beside a large oak tree.

"Hungry Heart, I have more for you. Come with me to the Second Mountain."

"But, Master, what about the robbers and the taskmasters? Can it be true?"

"Hungry Heart, keep your eyes on me. If you stay on the path and do not waver to the right or to the left, you will be safe. I have many things to show you and to teach you, but you must be willing to trust me in spite of what others may or may not experience. The choice is yours. You may stay here; you may go back. Or you may come and follow me."

Without another word, he continued the descent to the base of the mountain.

Hungry Heart quickly gathered up her paradigm pieces and ran after him, calling, "I am coming, Master, I am coming."

Now the Master moved more quickly—Hungry Heart didn't have time to be distracted. What a sight to see—the Master, with his long confident gait, and Hungry Heart running as fast as possible behind him. Every so often he called back over his shoulder with a hearty laugh, "Come on, Hungry Heart! You don't want to miss anything, do you?"

When they finally reached the foothills, a spectacular carpet of wildflowers stretched out between the two mountains. Travelers appeared from every direction and converged upon this field. There were so many travelers, in fact, that Hungry Heart had to walk on her tiptoes to keep the Master in view over the crowd.

At the entrance to the Second Mountain, one of the Master's assistants climbed to a tall golden platform held up by five golden pillars and asked everyone to sit down for orientation. The Master himself stood just behind the assistant and listened with everyone else.

"Welcome to the Second Mountain of the Master's Dwelling. The Master extends greetings and invites you to enter his service here. The Second Mountain serves the entire kingdom of Christianity. The Master's oil of enlightenment is burned here and the bread of his bounty is served here. The Second Mountain is a journey of service, much like the First Mountain. However, here you will learn to speak on his behalf and to use his authority.

"You all have come from many different places for many different reasons. Thus the Second Mountain is a place of diversity, and it must be approached as such. The Master has established the way, but the journey is yours. You will meet others who have their own unique journeys. You will hear many languages, learn different viewpoints, travel paths that often appear obscure, and meet hearts of every description.

"There are only two things that many of you will have in common on this journey. The first one is your love for the Master. Even this may often seem contradictory. If it does, it may challenge your love for one another. Second, you each will receive the designated apparel for the Second Mountain. This blue coat will fit over your white linen garment and will give you authority to travel anywhere within the borders of the Second Mountain and to speak on behalf of the Master.

"As always, you are free to stay as long as you like. If at any time you perceive that the journey is too difficult, you may return home. Do not be concerned about food and lodging. These will be provided for you as the need arises. The Master is a gracious host and will meet every need as long as you keep your eyes upon him."

At first Hungry Heart listened to the assistant and carefully watched for the Master's approval. After a few minutes, however, she grew so excited that her eyes, as well as her ears, fixed on the assistant instead of on the Master. The assistant's voice was smooth, reassuring, and convincing. Her heart fluttered just a tiny bit at his tall stance and handsome features. His dark eyes scanned the crowd as he spoke, and she was certain that he nodded several times in her direction.

Oh, it sounds so wonderful. I must learn as much as I possibly can here and maybe, just maybe, the Master will ask me to stay. Oh, perhaps one day, just perhaps, I can be one of his assistants here. This assistant is so wonderful! Surely he loves the Master as much as I do. His words are so eloquent. I must find out how he...

"Hungry Heart, the Master wants you to have this," the voice of a female assistant interrupted her thoughts. "It is the coat of authority, worn by all who journey on the Second Mountain. It will clothe you with the

Master's authority and remind everyone you meet that you represent him and serve him with your whole heart."

Hungry Heart accepted the blue coat with an appreciative smile, and the assistant slipped it over her head. Although everyone called it a "coat," it looked more like a seamless "cloak" with a long skirt. It completely covered her white garments. Her hands smoothed the silky linen fabric, and she picked up the hem to admire the delicate embroidered border. Red, blue, purple, and white thread formed clusters of grapes divided by tiny golden bells. After wearing white for so long, the warm vibrant colors gave her a sense of warmth, strength, and confidence, while the bells sounded a musical tribute to the Master every time she moved.

Each traveler received an identical blue coat. Some cheered with delight; others gave long thank-you speeches to the Master; and still others just smiled quietly. Little groups congregated as familiar hearts met one another and did everything from back slapping to hand clapping. It seemed, Hungry Heart noticed, that this new garment touched everyone's life differently.

Her own heart pounding with excitement, Hungry Heart found herself quietly singing a little song of thanksgiving as a sensation of loving warmth bathed her being. Tears of joy slipped from her eyes, and she wanted, more than anything, to thank the Master for granting her this beautiful gift. Although the precious blue coat covered the outside of her body, something new now covered her heart, something very different. Hungry Heart slipped to the side of the crowd for a clear view of the Master and started to make her way in his direction. He had not moved from his position behind his assistant, apparently waiting for the enthusiastic travelers to settle down.

"Have you been waiting a long time, Hungry Heart?"

An elderly searching heart's voice startled her, and she looked around. The woman appeared much too old and too frail to be climbing mountains. *Why,* thought Hungry Heart, *she looks older than Grandfather Humble Heart!* Yet here she was, dressed in the same blue coat of authority, and evidently ready to approach the Second Mountain. After a moment of surprise, Hungry Heart responded graciously, "No, I just arrived this morning. How long have you been here?"

The searching heart gazed ahead at the mountain in front of them. "I have been here for a very long time. When I arrived, I was a young girl, much like yourself, but I've been waiting…"

70

"Waiting for what?" Hungry Heart tried to show a sincere interest despite her anxiety to move on. She kept one eye on Searching Heart and one eye on the Master, who was now beginning to move on.

"For someone to show me the way in, to tell me what to say when I get there, to help me to do what needs to be done. I do not know how to proceed."

"But, you heard the assistant; we should just keep our eyes on the Master. He shows us the way, he tells us what to say, and he will help us to do what needs to be done."

"I know, and I should have followed him many years ago when I first received my coat. But the excitement and the joy right here was so wonderful. I couldn't leave. I just stayed, year after year, watching others come and go and receive their coats of authority. It is such a joyful place. I thought that I could be satisfied to stay here forever, but now I know that I must go on. I must...I simply must, but it has been so long since I've seen the Master or heard his voice. Oh, I know that he is there, but my eyes are dim, my ears do not hear as well as they used to, and my legs are feeble. Hungry Heart, would you help me? I may die right here without ever knowing the wonder of the Second Mountain."

Hungry Heart hesitated. On one hand she wanted to help the poor searching heart. On the other hand, she did not want to delay her own journey. If this woman could not see, how could she ever make it over the Second Mountain by herself? But then again, how had she made it this far? Surely there were assistants here who could help her.

Hungry Heart looked around in desperation. The crowd was moving underneath the tall golden platform and between the five pillars, taking little thought for the poor old woman or Hungry Heart's dilemma. Within a few minutes, the two stood there alone, still waiting for Hungry Heart to make up her mind. In her hesitation, she had lost sight of the Master. She had to hurry!

"If I help you through the gate and show you where the path is, will you be able to travel yourself? I have a long journey, and I do not believe that you will be able to keep up with me. What do you think?"

"Oh yes, just help me find my way through the gateway. If I die there, I will be content. Oh, thank you, Hungry Heart, thank you!"

Hungry Heart bit her lower lip in disappointment. If only the poor old woman had been gracious enough to decline her offer. They stepped forward through the golden gateway together, ever so slowly, one little step at a time.

CHAPTER II

Deception in the Harvest Fields

Eventually the two women found themselves standing at the outermost edge of sun-ripened wheat fields that stretched around the base of the entire Second Mountain like a golden wedding band. Men, women, and children, dressed in the blue robes of authority, moved through the fields bundling the wheat by hand and singing songs about the Master's bountiful harvest. Their songs reminded Hungry Heart of the weekly Celebration back on the Plains of Hope.

The workers waved and called out, "Come and join us! There's plenty of work for everyone!"

Hungry Heart wanted to get on with her journey, not stop to work in the fields. Her eyes scanned every direction for an alternate route. *This will only delay my trip up the mountain, but there appears to be no other way up. Besides, we can hardly pass through the fields without doing our share of the work.*

To complicate matters further, Hungry Heart failed to see the Master anywhere. She raised her voice as loudly as possible, "Master, where are you? Wait for us!"

Even Searching Heart helped her to call for him. "Master, show us the way!"

Much to their dismay, only silence answered their cries. Exasperated, Hungry Heart called over to the workers and inquired, "Have you seen the Master pass this way?"

"Oh yes, he was here, just as he is every morning. Come join us and you will see him tomorrow at first light."

"Well, I guess it's better than standing here until tomorrow or heading off in the wrong direction. We might as well help with the work," she decided finally.

Searching Heart started to protest, but Hungry Heart headed into the fields. In spite of her misgivings, Searching Heart followed as best she could, apologizing profusely for causing Hungry Heart to lose sight of the Master.

Before long, a real sense of camaraderie developed among everyone. They shared paradigm piece stories, adventures with the Master, and hopeful aspirations for the future. Hungry Heart enjoyed learning about planting, growing, and harvesting the wheat. The majority of the workers were diligent hearts, but not everyone. The precocious hearts seemed to know everything about farming, and the joyful hearts sang joyfully while they worked. Servant hearts brought buckets of cool water and tasty sandwiches at mealtime, and helpful hearts gave a hand wherever they were needed.

The religious hearts circled the workers from time to time, quoted from the Great Book, and admonished everyone to do their best. They spoke about the Master and his great love for the people of Christianity. Hungry Heart worked, sang, and feasted with the others. The next morning she watched in vain for the Master.

"Oh yes," everyone assured her, "he was here, and he will be back tomorrow."

The next day Hungry Heart missed him again, and the next, and the next. Searching Heart tried to keep watch as well, but the younger hearts were always in the way or making too much noise for her to hear his voice.

On the sixth day, a young man arrived unexpectedly.

"The Master has sent me to oversee the harvest," he said. "I will evaluate the work schedule and reassign your duties. We must work together like a well-oiled machine for the Master. If you'll do as I say, the harvest will be in before you know it!"

Work ceased everywhere at the sound of his voice. The joyful hearts stopped singing, and the servant hearts dropped their baskets.

"I do not believe the Master would do that," protested a precocious heart boldly. "The Master shows us how to work the fields. He already has given us assignments, so why should he change them now? This does not make sense. Who is this stranger?"

The worker hearts laughed at the questions and welcomed the stranger into their midst.

"We are happy to have everyone who wants to work with us. Certainly, if you have experience and the Master has sent you, we welcome your supervision. Yes, some reorganization might increase our production and help us to meet our harvest deadline."

Searching Heart quietly pulled at her friend's sleeve. "Hungry Heart, we must be careful. He looks like one of us because he wears the blue coat of authority, but I think his heart is strange. I am not sure...." her voice trailed off when the strange heart glanced in her direction with an accusing look.

Hungry Heart watched him curiously as the young man mingled with the others. *This is most strange,* she thought. *One moment he is a worker heart, and the next moment he is a servant heart. Then he becomes a joyful heart and attempts to teach us new songs. Who is he and where did he come from?*

The young man caught her watching him and stopped to meet her.

"Hungry Heart! I am so glad to see you here. You and I are so much alike you know—we are both hungry to learn about the Master. We are going to get on quite well, you and I, and we will have this field cleared in no time at all."

Surprised and somewhat flattered, Hungry Heart just nodded in agreement and listened to his harvest plan. He asked her to sit down with him. Slowly, in a serious tone, he said,

"I know that you have been here only a short time, but I also know that your hungry heart learns things quickly. You can help me by sharing some of the things you have learned about the rest of the workers here."

He ran his hands over his blue coat and reminded her, "The Master counts on me, you know. I have a great responsibility here, and he is also counting on you to help me."

He went on to ask her about this one and that one, carefully pointing out that everything she shared would be held in the strictest confidence. Eager to receive his approval, she lovingly pointed out the limitations of her friend Searching Heart's age and dim eyesight, the well-intended but overbearing attitude of the worker hearts and the exasperation of the precocious hearts. She warned him that the servant hearts often looked down on everyone else and that there were a few jealous hearts in the midst. On and on, he probed her mind. When her supply of relevant information exhausted itself, he excused himself.

"Well, it's getting late. I must meet with the worker hearts and plan our strategy for tomorrow. You have been most helpful. I will have a special assignment for you, just you wait and see."

When he left, Hungry Heart had an uncomfortable feeling in the pit of her stomach. She felt almost as if he had stolen something very precious from her, but what was it? After all, the Master had sent him, and he had asked for her help. How could she have refused? She watched him move over to join the worker hearts. Within minutes they were all in deep conversation. From time to time they glanced her way and nodded to each other.

"Hungry Heart, are you all right? You look ill."

Searching Heart touched her shoulder lightly in concern and then tried to follow Hungry Heart's gaze to the group of worker hears huddled with the stranger heart.

"What is it? What did he say to you?"

"I don't know, but I think I've done something—something very foolish—and I must find the Master quickly. Have you seen him?"

"No, not since the gateway. It's most distressing. There has been so much to do. I had hoped that you had seen him. My eyes are getting weaker each day."

"Shh. The stranger heart is coming over here again."

"Well, Hungry Heart, look who's here. Why, I do declare, this must be your friend Searching Heart herself. I have heard so much about you, Searching Heart," he said, sneaking a quick glance in Hungry Heart's direction. "Well, I am glad that both of you are here. It will save me time. Tomorrow, I want the two of you to take over the responsibilities of the servant hearts. I have something else for them, and you two can serve at mealtimes. It is a great responsibility, but I know that I can count on the two of you. Right? After all, we do not want to disappoint the Master."

Speechless, they shook their heads in confused agreement.

The next day the hearts reported to their new assignments. Everyone tried their best, but they fell further and further behind. The harder they tried to please the new supervisor, the less work they accomplished, and the angrier he became. By noon he pulled out a long black whip and cracked it in the air as he shouted, "Work harder! Work for the Master, or he will abandon you to the Land of the Lost! You will lose your paradigm pieces and your citizenship in Christianity! I have never seen such sluggards! Work!"

Hungry Heart froze in her tracks. She remembered Sacrificial Heart's admonition about working so hard to please the Master when all that he wanted from her was the brokenness in her own life. Suddenly Hungry Heart realized that the stranger was a "deceiving heart," one who comes as a friend, but has dark underlying motives.

Why didn't I recognize him before? How could I have been duped into believing him? Desperately she looked around for Searching Heart. She soon found her slumped over a large water bucket, crying.

"I can't see to carry the buckets any longer. I am nearly blind. I have failed the Master, and I will be sent to the Land of the Lost!"

"Nonsense! We are not going to lose anything. What we are going to do is to get out of here—and fast! That stranger is a deceptive heart! He is not going to beat us into believing his lies. Get up and take my hand. We've got to find the Master!"

As soon as the stranger turned his back, the two women seized their opportunity and ran as fast as they could. Hand in hand they headed north through the fields, crying out, "Master, help, please show us the way!" Miraculously, Searching Heart ran with the speed and agility of a young woman. Her feeble legs grew stronger with each leap. It wasn't long before Hungry Heart saw the Master just ahead, smiling, as if he had been waiting for them all along.

"Oh, Master, you won't believe it! A deceptive heart pretended to be your servant! And he cracked a long whip! He turned everyone against each other. And Searching Heart can barely see, but he had no mercy! You will do something, won't you? Surely you won't allow him to continue?"

"Hungry Heart, did I ask you to go into the fields?" Ashamed, she lowered her eyes and shook her head. He continued, "Did I ask you to stay there and work?"

Searching Heart stepped forward and stood between the two of them.

"Please, Master, it was my fault. I slowed Hungry Heart down at the gate and she lost sight of you. If you are angry, be angry with me, not her. I am too old and too blind to travel, but she must continue her journey to complete her paradigm."

A tear slipped from the Master's eye, and he allowed it to fall on Searching Heart's head as he reached out for her hand.

"You have shown great love today. Although your eyes are dim, your heart has keen vision. Will you serve me in the Village of Enlightenment?"

Surprised and excited, Searching Heart could barely contain herself. Falling to her knees, she thanked the Master for even considering her for such an assignment. He graciously acknowledged her delight and then turned his attention to Hungry Heart.

"Now, I want you to help Searching Heart find her way to the Village of Enlightenment. I will lead the way, but you must be her eyes until she reaches the village. Will you do this for me?"

She bit her lower lip and nodded, thankful for the opportunity to prove her faithfulness. "But, Master, what about the deceptive heart in the fields?"

Never turning around to acknowledge her question, he stepped forward and reminded her, "Hungry Heart, follow me."

Following the Master, Hungry Heart held Searching Heart by the hand as they traveled up and around the mountainside. Fortunately it was a short journey, and soon they stood on a high buff overlooking the Village of Enlightenment. Tall magnificent lamp stands surrounded the perimeter of the village and lined the streets. Although daylight still covered the mountain, the village itself glowed with warm iridescent hues of golden light. Even the sunlight paled in comparison to the radiance from the lamp stands.

"Oh, my friend, how I wish you could see this beautiful sight," Hungry Heart whispered to Searching Heart in awe.

CHAPTER 12

The Village of Enlightenment

The sloping northern mountainside embraced the village like a protective mother's arms. Clusters of small adobe dwellings filled secluded alcoves while lamp stands towered above the highest rooftops, coloring the entire village with golden hues. Even the Master paused to appreciate the atmosphere surrounding the village before he spoke.

"Very special lights burn in this village day and night. Faithful servants work to fill the street lamps that light not only the eyes, but also the heart. Searching Heart, this is your new home. This is also the end of your search, your place of appointment. Will you serve me here as a lamp keeper, to light the way for travelers?"

Still unable to see the village or fully comprehend his words, Searching Heart fell at his feet and wept. For the first time in her life, the joy of contentment filled her heart. Despite the years she had chosen to remain at the gateway to the Second Mountain, the Master had sent Hungry Heart into her life so she could find her way here. He patiently waited for her tearful release, then motioned both of them to follow him down to the village.

When they reached the center of the village, the Master introduced them to one of his assistant lamp keepers. These particular assistants monitored the golden lamp stands and kept them filled day and night. People gathered under these spectacular iridescent circles of light to read the Great Book. The assistant lamp keeper placed an open copy of the Book in Searching Heart's hand, and she tried to politely refuse.

"Oh no, thank you. My eyes are dim and unable to see as they used to..."

Before she finished speaking, her eyes fell on the pages in front of her. Her lips trembled in excitement.

"Oh, oh, oh, what is this? I can see...the words...I can read them...this light... it must be a miracle!" She looked up at the lamp keeper in wonder as he turned the pages and explained.

"The Master's light has special qualities. Travelers come from far away just to sit under his lights and read the Master's Great Book. Even those who have keen eyesight see things they have never seen before. Reading the Great Book without the Master's light is like walking without feet."

Searching Heart stopped listening and sat down to read, but Hungry Heart wanted to know more.

"Where does the lamp oil come from? I have never seen fire produce a light such as this. How does it illuminate the Great Book?"

"The Master sends the precious oil from his olive groves and oil presses just outside the village," the lamp keeper explained. "This oil produces white-hot flames, yet the fire glows with the Master's gentle love and creates rainbows of light over the pages of the Great Book. No one except the Master knows exactly how it works—that it works is enough."

Not far away, a white-haired faithful heart looked up from his copy of the Great Book, smiled directly at Hungry Heart, and agreed.

"The longer you remain under the light, the more you will be able to comprehend the incomprehensible, although you will not be able to express it because it is inexpressible," he said.

With that, the Master placed his hand on Hungry Heart's shoulder and said, "Searching Heart will come with me to begin her training, but I want you to remain here under the lamps of enlightenment."

"Of course, Master, but for how long?"

"Until you see the light burning in your heart."

The Master's words puzzled Hungry Heart. How could the light possibly burn in her heart? It burned from the lamp stands. However, before she could ask him anything else, a friendly heart invited her to join a group underneath a nearby lamp stand.

"Welcome to the Village of Enlightenment, Hungry Heart. We are always thrilled to have hungry hearts because you are eager and willing to learn everything you can about the Master. Why don't you join our study group? We have an empty seat over here."

At the Master's nod of approval, Hungry Heart followed Friendly

Heart. Some of the group sat on the ground, others occupied circular benches around the lamp stand base, and still others stood. Everyone, though, held a copy of the Great Book in his or her hands. There were a good number in the group, more than Hungry Heart could count in a quick glance. Still they made room for her on one of the benches, encouraged her to sit down, and handed her a copy of the Great Book. This copy was small and convenient for traveling, unlike the one she had left back on the Plains of Hope.

For some reason lost in time-honored traditions, everyone on the Plains of Hope owned a large, heavy copy of the Great Book—the larger the better. Grandfather Humble Heart's was so big it sat on a large stand in his living room. Her parents had given her one several years ago, but she kept it in her bedroom because it was too cumbersome to carry around. Besides, every meeting place seemed to have their own unique version, and it was easier to use the ones there than to argue about the differences.

Here, however, no one appeared to care about the size, color, or variety. Hungry Heart ran her hands lovingly over the small white book and realized that it fit perfectly into a small pocket in her blue coat of authority.

Every day in the weeks that followed, Hungry Heart sat under the lamp stand with her new friends. Since the light burned day and night, no one kept regular daytime hours. If one grew sleepy, he slept. If someone became hungry, he stopped to eat from baskets of fresh fruit, vegetables, and bread, which the servant hearts kept filled for the travelers.

Everyone read the Great Book, always showing great appreciation for the reflections and revelations they found there. Each one held the Master's name in the highest esteem, giving him honor at every possible opportunity. The group reminded Hungry Heart of the Celebrations and the meeting places on the Plains of Hope. Yet, instead of one elder expounding great knowledge, everyone shared insights. Above all, the Master stayed close at hand. Sometimes he stopped by to check their progress; other times he attended to business in the village itself, unless someone called on him. However, he could always be seen—even from a great distance.

Held up to the light, paradigm pieces became objects of unsurpassed beauty. The symbolic pieces were beautiful anywhere, yet here their beauty exceeded everyone's expectations. The slightest movement, under the rainbow of light, gave each piece a new dimension and a new shade of meaning. One by one, the group members stepped to the center of the circle, directly under the lamp stand, and shared their paradigm stories.

As the newest member of the group, Hungry Heart waited patiently until someone announced, "It is time to hear from Hungry Heart."

Hungry Heart stepped to the center of the circle, directly under the lamp stand, and removed the paradigm pouch from over her heart. Several travelers murmured in appreciation at the blue pouch filled with paradigm pieces of many shapes and colors. From the number of pieces Hungry Heart poured out, it was obvious that she had been to many places and had received much truth.

She chose her favorite, the tiny golden flame from the refinery, held it up to the light and pronounced loudly, "The Master's flame of love burns in my heart. His fire consumes everything in my life that I do not need."

Heads nodded in agreement while a studious religious heart recited from the Great Book, "The Master has said, 'Everything that does not produce life must be consumed.'"

No one, except the Master of course, really knows how long Hungry Heart remained under the lamp stand of enlightenment reading from the Great Book. She spent the majority of her time there, hungry for every word of truth and revelation. Sometimes she stopped to help other travelers find a seat or assisted the lamplighters with their tasks. On occasion, Searching Heart stopped by to visit for a few minutes and share one of her new adventures as a lamp keeper trainee.

From time to time, the Master's assistants asked Hungry Heart to read aloud from the Great Book—a great honor indeed. Gradually she found herself actually reciting its pages from memory with confidence and ease. The words poured from her heart when she opened her mouth to speak, and many travelers began to seek her out for encouragement. The Master stopped by several times a day to answer her questions or to direct her to a new section of the Great Book.

On each occasion, he asked, "Hungry Heart, what do you see?" and she eagerly shared her new insights. One day, at his usual question, she repeated some insights she had heard from a studious heart in an earlier conversation. The Master ignored her reply and repeated, "Hungry Heart, what do *you* see?" Clearly, he wanted to hear her own heart speak, not someone else's.

In the beginning, their conversations always concluded with Hungry Heart's question, "How long must I remain here, Master?" However, as time passed, the contentment in her heart increased. Eventually she stopped thinking about her journey to the Third Mountain and began to consider herself a permanent resident in the Village of Enlightenment. She and Searching Heart shared a quaint little room in one of the adobe dwellings, and she traveled from lamp stand to lamp stand to greet fellow travelers, to listen, to read, to recite, and to give a helping hand wherever she was needed. Her hungry heart enjoyed the diversity of these experiences, and she felt quite at home. The Master never indicated it, but Hungry Heart started to believe that she, like Searching Heart, had found her place of appointment.

One afternoon the lamp keepers did not arrive at the scheduled time to trim the wicks and refill the large lamp bases with oil. The people began to murmur, and then the murmurs turned to grumbles. From there the grumbles turned to rumbles. Soon the entire village erupted in confusion. A few fearful hearts expressed concerns.

"Where are the lamp keepers? We shall be swallowed up in the darkness if we cannot read the Great Book. The spirit creatures will deceive our hearts and lead us to the Land of the Lost..."

On and on, voices arose until no one could be heard reading from the Great Book at all. To make matters worse, the growing darkness prevented them from seeing the Master.

Hungry Heart watched the flickering lamp stands and stepped back as large, dark-winged creatures circled the flickering lights. They looked like giant dragonflies with bright green eyes, and their wings hummed with the noise of a swarm of giant bees.

"It's the creatures! Look, they have wings!" someone screamed in terror.

Hungry Heart tried to hide the fear growing in her own heart, but the flying creatures grew bolder and bolder. In no time at all they were everywhere—in the air, on the benches, and clinging to the lamp stands. Travelers ran from them, beat them away, and even used copies of the Great Book to swat at them. People cried in pain from a slight touch of their scale-covered wings, and Hungry Heart ducked away just in time as a large dark ugly wing tip soared in her direction.

"Master! Master! Help us!" One fearful heart after another cried out until everyone called upon him at once.

"We will perish without the light, and the darkness will consume us! We need oil, Master, we need oil! Please, have pity on us! This is your village…send the lamp keepers to fill the lamps! The spirit creatures are too powerful for us…please help us!"

Now the lamp keepers were attempting to make their way to the lamp stands, but the confused and fearful hearts pushed and fought them until they had no choice but to stand back, lest they spill the precious oil.

Finally a courageous heart spoke with great authority and announced above the chaos, "Make way! Make way! The lamp keepers are here with oil. Allow them to pass. The Master has heard our cries and the evil ones will be defeated."

At the sound of this declaration, Hungry Heart stepped aside with the others to create a clear path to the nearest lamp stand. The winged creatures buzzed about their heads, but the lamp keepers did not waver from their task. They filled the tall lamps and, within moments, the village once again stood aglow with the soft warm light. Repelled by the light, the dreadful intruders disappeared into the distance.

"What did you see, Hungry Heart?" The Master asked softly with his hand on her shoulder.

A long, somewhat uncomfortable silence followed his question. Then slowly, as if still attempting to understand the conflict, she answered him, "The light not only helps us to read and understand the Great Book, it also protects us. Without it, we are helpless against the creatures of darkness. They moved so fast and created confusion so quickly that no one had time to consider what he should or should not do. Master, you told us to never allow the light to grow dim, yet oil did not come in time. I do not understand. The only thing I could see were the giant flies, their terrible wings, and their hateful eyes."

The Master nodded in silent understanding, then added, "Hungry Heart, you understand the beauty and the covering that the light provides for you. You have seen the dangers of darkness, as well as your dependence upon someone else to provide the oil. What else do you see?"

"I see that I must stay close to the lamp stand, make certain that it is filled with oil and never, never allow the light to grow dim."

"Yes, this is a possibility; however, if you do this, my child, you will never be able to continue your journey, will you? As always, the choice is yours."

Hungry Heart hung her head in shame, realizing not only the insufficiency of her answer, but also that she had forgotten the journey ahead of her.

"But, Master, how will I ever be able to continue my journey to the Third Mountain? The lamp stands are here, and the Third Mountain is very far away."

"You will be able to travel just as soon as the light burns brightly in your own heart."

Without another word, he stepped aside to address a group of curious hearts standing by waiting for him. Hungry Heart watched him silently, wondering when and if she would ever understand his words. They sounded more like a riddle, and she fought back the temptation to believe that this was all some kind of impossible test.

After her frightful experience with the evil spirit creatures, Hungry Heart stayed close to the lamp stand and diligently searched the Great Book for revelation. There were many references to light and darkness and hearts, but she still found it difficult to understand. She began to move from one lamp stand to the next, asking one person after another, "How does the light burn brightly in my heart?"

Everyone appeared to have a different answer. By this time, she had learned that the lamp keepers were very territorial. Each believed their lamp stand to be the best and safest. More than once she received stern warnings.

"You must stay here, close to *this* lamp stand. Do not attempt to travel from one to another. You will find yourself wandering from place to place and confusion will fill your heart. You will lose your position, and you will need to reestablish yourself again and again. Here we know you, and we want you to encourage others. You have many gifts to give, Hungry Heart, but you must learn how to settle your heart. When you do, the light will burn brightly within you for all to see."

A few religious hearts encouraged her to be more diligent about reading from the Great Book: "The degree of light in your heart depends upon your knowledge of the Great Book."

"You must join the dance and celebrate as often as possible," the joyful hearts counseled her.

She tried to follow everyone's counsel until one day she just gave up. That day, the Master found her sitting on a large rock at the very edge of the village, just barely under the light.

"Hungry Heart, what do you see today?"

Frustrated and tired of trying to answer the Master's apparent riddle, she blurted out, "I see a village filled with lamp stands that glow with indescribable beauty and illuminate the Great Book in ways that I did not dare to imagine before. I see so many circles of light that it is impossible for me to sit under each one, or even to remain under one and forget the others. I see untold numbers of travelers who are rejoicing in the gifts and provisions of the lamp stands. They are growing in their knowledge of you and the Great Book. They are learning to speak and walk with authority and confidence. Yet the longer I stay here, the less confident I become. The more I learn, the less I know."

The look in her eyes and the tenseness of her body said it all as she raised her voice in desperation.

"I want to please you and I want the light to burn in my heart, but, Master, I do not want to sit under lamp stands any longer. I have failed to find the light in my own heart. You want the light to burn in my heart, but I cannot do it. I have asked everyone and tried everything. I simply cannot do whatever it is you are asking of me. I have tried, and I am tired of trying. I feel strange and confused! Unkind thoughts about the lamp keepers and the other travelers are beginning to eat away at me like hungry locusts. I escaped from the winged spirits, but I cannot escape from the shadows in my own heart, even here in the Village of Enlightenment!"

Hungry Heart looked away from the Master and closed her eyes, ashamed of her frustration and indignant tone. Never had she dared to speak to him with such disrespect. Would he send her away, back to the Plains of Hope? Opening her eyes, she stared silently at the Village of Enlightenment until the tightness in her body relaxed. Someplace, deep inside her heart, burned an unquenchable love. Then she looked up at the Master, as if for the very first time.

"You, Master, are the only one who lights the way for me. Without you, I am lost and destined to walk in the shadows alone. The village is beautiful, and I am thankful that you have given me the opportunity to stay here—but it cannot compare with the fire that burns in my heart when I am with you. Forgive me, please. I need you, and I do want to continue my journey to the Third Mountain."

He smiled and reached for her hand. "Hungry Heart, it is time for you to continue your journey. You have seen the darkness of your own heart and allowed the light of my love to overcome it. You are the lamp keeper of your heart, and you know where to find the oil. I have all you need. Keep the flame of love burning day and night. This paradigm piece will remind you that the light in your heart will illuminate, guide, and teach you as you continue your journey."

His touch brought a warmth into her hand that tingled all the way up her arm. Even after he stepped back and released her hand, the heat radiated in her palm from a small, golden, pear-shaped gemstone. It would always remind her that the light of the Master's love burned in her heart. The Master gave her a few moments to appreciate her new paradigm piece, then urged, "Hurry now, we have a long way to go."

CHAPTER 13

Dangerous Distractions

Obediently, Hungry Heart followed the Master south through the forest to a road, which led through wide meadows and small camp settlements. To Hungry Heart's surprise, out in the fields on either side of the well-traveled route, men and women argued loudly, poked at each other with long rods, and pulled at one another's garments. Here and there small groups banded together around campfires, forbidding anyone to approach their personal circles unless they recited vows of loyalty to the group itself.

The majority of these people bore a striking resemblance to warrior hearts, but Hungry Heart realized that something was amiss. Warrior hearts were known not only for their courage and fierceness in battle, but also for their allegiance to the Master's army. They did not turn on one another like this or separate from the main ranks.

"Master, who are these people? Why are they fighting, here on your Second Mountain?"

The Master sighed as he glanced from side to side as they passed by.

"These hearts have journeyed as far as the Village of Enlightenment, just as you did, and enjoyed great love for one another. They love me and they love the Great Book, but they also love something else, something very harmful—they love to contend for their place of authority. Their pride has enticed their hearts to turn away from the path. Regardless of what they once were, they are now rebellious hearts."

Hungry Heart stared at the rebellious hearts in disbelief. How can the Master tolerate such behavior on his mountain? Even citizens on the Plains of Hope shunned rebellious hearts until they recognized the error of their ways. Nobody wanted to be found with a rebellious heart because rebellion against the Master often led to banishment in the Land of the Lost.

"But, Master, why do you allow this to continue?"

"This is their journey, and they have choices to make, just as you do," he answered with the same serious tone he used so often, the one that reminded her to concentrate on her own journey and to keep her eyes on him.

"Oh, Master, I will follow you wherever you lead me. My heart belongs to you and you alone," Hungry Heart declared emphatically. She shook her head in disappointment at the misguided hearts surrounding them and smoothed out her own blue coat of authority with pride.

The Master smiled and accepted her pledge of loyalty while motioning for her to step carefully around two rebellious hearts. They were slapping each other with copies of the Great Book and shouting personal insults back and forth, each claiming to have heard a greater truth from the Master.

Hungry Heart and the Master witnessed more skirmishes to the right and to the left, and sometimes even on the roadway itself, but no one interrupted them until about sundown.

For just a short span of time, the heavens and earth embraced each other in a spectacular blend of yellow and red in the western sky. Hungry Heart stared at the incredibly breathtaking view, unable to see where the mountains ended and the sky began. And just for a moment, she took her eyes from the Master.

Before Hungry Heart could turn her eyes back to the road, she stumbled into three travelers. The unexpected encounter knocked her off the narrow roadway and into a patch of brambles. The sharp thorns pierced her flesh, and she cried out at the sight of her bloody hands.

"Hungry Heart, are you hurt? Come, let me help you," one of the travelers offered compassionately. "Please forgive us for blocking the path. We were discussing our strategy to defeat the dragon, and we didn't see you coming."

The heart pulled her safely back to the path, and his two companions bandaged her wounds with long white cloths from their mercy baskets. Looking up, she recognized the man and his two companions as bold hearts, fearless and ready to face any danger that might arise.

"The dragon? On the Master's mountain? Oh no, you must be mistaken. That is quite impossible. The dragon lives in the Land of the Lost and dwells in the seas of darkness," Hungry Heart protested.

Old country folklore described a dragon-like monster with an insatiable hunger for any form of life—trees, shrubs, animals, and even men. However, no one on the Plains of Hope, or even in all of Christianity, had reason to fear it because it lived far beyond Christianity's borders and did not dare approach the Master's domain. No, these bold hearts were definitely misinformed, and Hungry Heart did her best to correct them. Despite her rebuke, they persisted with bold confidence.

"Didn't the Master tell you? Oh, you poor hungry heart, didn't anyone at all tell you about the dragon's power? You have been to the Village of Enlightenment and had your eyes opened. Now you will see things you have never seen before. You will see the creature roaming the earth looking for unsuspecting prey."

"But," one bold heart interjected loudly, "the Master has given you his authority to use against it. Just ask the Master for yourself if you don't believe us. You're wearing his coat of authority just as we are."

Confused, Hungry Heart looked at the Master, who had been waiting patiently for her attention. "What are they talking about, Master?"

With a slight nod he confirmed their words. "It is true, Hungry Heart; you now have eyes to see and ears to hear many things you did not see or hear before. Here, on the Second Mountain, you will learn to use my authority. The dragon does not dare to violate my authority; however, he is free to roam, even here on the Second Mountain."

"But, Master, I have never seen him on the Plains of Hope, on the Mountains of Faith, in the Cities of Abiding Love or even down in the Valley of Despair. How can he be here on your mountain?"

"You did not see him, Hungry Heart, because you did not have eyes to see. Now you do, but do not be afraid. You have something else. You wear the blue coat of authority, and I have given you permission to speak in my name. What's more, you also have my promises from the Great Book. It records great battles and victories over the dragon, as well as the weapons and strategies that undermine its power."

"No one told me...no one ever read from the Great Book about this creature..." She fumbled for words to explain her apparent lack of knowledge.

"No, it is not that no one read about it from the Great Book. It is simply that you did not have ears to hear. Do not cast blame on others for the lack in your own life. Here, I will show you."

Hungry Heart and the bold hearts sat down with the Master at a roadside resting area. He opened his own small, golden copy of the Great Book and read to them about the presence, dangers, and limitations of the fire-breathing dragon. He described the dragon, which had armor-like scales on its back and made the earth shake with its footsteps. The bold hearts murmured in agreement while Hungry Heart listened in near disbelief.

She had learned about and seen the evil spirit creatures from time to time, but they were mischievous troublemakers in comparison with this monster. Exactly why the Master permitted him access here, he did not say or attempt to explain. Instead, he finished reading and stood up, obviously indicating that it was time to continue the journey.

"But, Master," one of the bold hearts protested, "it is nearly dark, and we do not have any shelter here. It is best that we find a place to make camp for the night. Of course, we are not afraid of the dragon or the darkness. However, the dragon is in the area, and we should stay here to face him at first light."

The Master acknowledged the bold hearts' comments, then turned directly to Hungry Heart. "What are you going to do? Do you want to continue the journey with me now, or do you want to join the bold hearts in their camp?"

The bold hearts do make a good point, she reasoned to herself; but before she could answer the Master, he disappeared down the road from her sight. It was almost as if he had known all along what her answer would be.

Seeing the panic in her eyes, the tallest bold heart assured her, "Don't worry, this is all part of the journey and the test we have to face. Look, just ahead is a good place to make camp. We will build a big fire, set up our tents, and take turns on watch throughout the night. Tomorrow we will fight and use the Master's authority to destroy the dragon on our way into the city."

"But the Master wants me to keep my eyes on him."

"You can make up for lost time tomorrow," the bold heart reassured her. "Besides, you are in good hands. We've trained under strong warrior hearts, and we know the countryside. In fact, I believe the Master arranged this meeting, don't you? It seems as if we were destined to find each other."

Yes, Hungry Heart conceded, *it did appear that way.* After all, the Master did not stop the meeting or warn her in any way. Certainly it would be much safer to stay with her new friends than to venture out alone. She refused to dwell on the fact that she had failed to answer the Master and went to sleep expecting to see him in the morning just as usual.

Despite her confidence, the next morning they traveled for hours without seeing the Master. One distraction after another interrupted the journey. Fellow travelers stopped them to talk, to share paradigm pieces, or to ask for directions. Her three companions, true bold hearts, tried to settle disputes, offer strategies and warn everyone about the dragon. All of this slowed Hungry Heart's own journey to a snail's pace and completely frustrated her.

By noon, uninterested in their personal endeavors and eager to catch up with the Master, Hungry Heart decided to move on ahead without the bold hearts, stopping only for short periods of rest. At first, the thought of traveling alone was unsettling. It reminded her of the North Wind and her search for Grandfather Humble Heart.

Since that time, or so it seemed, the Master had always provided her with traveling companions like Loving Heart, Sacrificial Heart, and Searching Heart. The workers at the Great Refinery and the assistants at the Lagoon of Truth on the First Mountain had helped her so much. She looked forward to seeing them again on her return home. Turning around, she hoped to catch one last glimpse of the Village of Enlightenment, but she had traveled too far and could no longer see the tall glowing lamp stands.

The thought of Searching Heart serving the Master as a lamp keeper made her smile. Who could have guessed the Master's plan for her? Or, for that matter, for any of her companions? Then again, why did she have to continually leave such special friends behind? *Oh, how I wish we could all travel to the Third Mountain together,* she sighed wistfully. *I can hardly believe how much the Master has taught me. I thought I knew him all those years on the Plains of Hope, but I am just beginning to know who he really is. He is so much more than the Master of Christianity. He is...*

Just then an indescribable, deep growl followed by screams and shouts startled her. Over to her left, down in a low sloping grassy meadow, crowds of people shouted, ran in every direction, sounded trumpets, waved swords, and cried out in terror. As the cloud of dust settled and the large group retreated, an ugly, black-scaled dragon reared its head and slapped its enormous arrow-shaped tail in retaliation.

Her heart almost stopped beating. Never had Hungry Heart seen anything so indescribably hideous—and so powerful! Stretching its long neck out and upward, the creature towered over the band of travelers as if they were harmless pests. She wanted to run, but her feet remained frozen in fear, glued to the earth. Blue-coated men, women and even children fought against the creature. A few ran away, but most of them stood their ground and tried to keep the dragon at bay. In their efforts to contain the dragon, the circle of people around it grew wider, soon reaching Hungry Heart's frozen position.

At first the people stepped around her, but within a few moments someone noticed her lack of involvement and shouted to her, "How can you just stand there? This is war! You are wearing the Master's blue coat of authority just as we are, so you have a responsibility to help us. If the monster overcomes us, we are all lost."

"But I have no weapons..." she protested weakly, shrinking back and looking around for a way out of the fight.

"You are here now, and you must do your part! You are a hungry heart. Use the hunger in your heart to overcome. Shout! Shout your hunger for victory! Be strong and courageous in your service for the Master! Shout until you are so hungry for victory that you won't stop until you have it!"

His words ignited her determination. "Yes! I want victory," she cried. "We will defeat the dragon!"

She forgot her fear, raised her voice, and moved forward with the others, waving her arms in every direction. From afar she had been able to see the enemy, but now in the confusion she lost sight of his thick scales and deep green eyes. Instead, a cloud of dust and flashes of silver swords surrounded her.

Everyone shouted in unison, "This mountain belongs to the Master! Go away, or we will stomp you under our feet."

Suddenly, a misguided sword struck her leg, hard. Hurt, she stumbled into an old man and fell to the ground. He glared at her with contempt and raised his sword in front of her face.

"Get out of my way! Go on, get out of my way, you idiot! You do not know how to fight. I have been in this battle for years, and I will not have you in my way.... You do not belong here, and you will be responsible if we perish!"

Stunned and bleeding, Hungry Heart crawled away from the battlefield before she finally fainted near some shrubs. There an entourage of mercy hearts found her. Mercy hearts were constantly scouring the field for the wounded, bandaging them and moving them to a nearby cave. Using their own coats to make a litter, they carried the unconscious Hungry Heart to their makeshift hospital cave.

When Hungry Heart regained consciousness, her eyes opened to see small torches hanging from the cavern walls, casting flickering shadows across wounded hearts that lay everywhere. Mercy hearts moved quietly from pallet to pallet, offering healing herbs, changing bandages, and spooning warm broth into mouths. Except for sounds of occasional weeping and the rustling of the caregivers going back and forth, the cave was quiet. One could sense the intense longing for the Master in the air, but no one had the strength to even whisper his name.

Hungry Heart smiled weakly at the mercy heart taking care of her and asked, "Who are you? What happened? Why is everyone here…and where is the Master?"

"I am Mercy Heart, and I have been assigned to take care of you until you are well enough to travel. Do you feel like sitting up? Perhaps a little warm broth might be just what you need. Be patient now. You have plenty of time to…"

"Tell me…what happened?" Hungry Heart interrupted. "How did I get here? How did all of these people get here?"

Mercy Heart hesitated at first, but when it was clear that Hungry Heart wouldn't eat or rest without answers, she did her best to explain.

"Hungry Heart, you allowed yourself to get caught up in what we call an 'unauthorized siege.'"

"A what?"

"An unauthorized siege is a fight that is not under the Master's authority. When we depend upon our own strategies and skills instead of his, the ranks of authority break down and we end up hurting each other instead of the enemy. Let me ask you this: Why did you join the battle?"

Hungry Heart's head ached and her leg throbbed, but she strained to remember. "While I was traveling along I saw the dragon and a large crowd trying to fight it. I didn't really know what to do, but so many people kept crying for me to help that I had to do something... Now I remember! Someone told me to shout! I shouted until somebody's sword hit my leg and I fell... That's about all I remember. Oh, where is the Master? I need to see him…I never should have taken my eyes from him."

Mercy Heart tucked a warm blanket around Hungry Heart with a soft assurance, "The Master is here, just as he always is when you need him.

However, you have been badly wounded, and you are not able to see or hear him as you are used to doing. As soon as you regain your strength, you will be able to discuss these matters with him. Right now, just rest, and allow me to take care of you."

"But why did they get angry at me? Those men...they turned on me...and..." Hungry Heart weakly protested.

"Shhh, it's time to rest. There will be plenty of time for answers later. Here, put your hand over your paradigm pieces and think about the things you already know instead of the things you do not know."

Mercy Heart took Hungry Heart's hand and placed it on the blue pouch still hanging over her heart.

Thankfully closing her eyes, Hungry Heart fingered the precious paradigm pieces through the fabric. She remembered as many as she could from far back in her childhood.

I am a citizen of Christianity and the Master loves me.

The Great Book tells me about his love.

Songs from the Mountain of Joy keep my heart centered in his love.

His truth will always guide me.

The Master's love burns away everything I do not need.

Mother, Father and Grandfather—the Master needs them.

I can swim like a fish in his truth, and his truth keeps my heart clean.

His love never fails.

One day I will receive my completed paradigm and

my place of appointment in his service.

All I need to do is to call upon the Master, and he will come.

On and on she recalled paradigm truth until a gentle hand touched her forehead. Drifting off into a restful sleep, she knew the Master had touched her.

CHAPTER 14

The Master's Authority

Day and night, the mercy hearts tended to wounded hearts. Some regained their strength and left, while new ones continued to find their way to the cave or be carried in on stretchers. A few families stayed with their wounded relatives in stunned silence, unable to believe the seemingly cruel treatment from long-time friends and allies in the fight against the dragon.

Deep in her dreams, Hungry Heart played on the Plains of Hope with her friends and family. She climbed the Mountains of Faith and sang with the joyful hearts on the Mountains of Joy. Then, in spite of her hopeful spirit, she dreamed that she fell from a high mountain peak and plunged into her deepest fears. Haunting images of dark shadows and hideous flying creatures chased her through misty nightmares. Lost and alone, she tried to cry out for help.

One scene after another flashed through the chambers of her subconscious as the North Wind blew away everyone she loved and trusted. At one point, Grandfather reached out for her, then disappeared into the mist. She watched Loving Heart teaching the children and tried to run to her friend, but her legs grew weaker and weaker. Her parents called to her from the Valley of Despair, and the spirit creatures laughed at her feeble attempts to answer them.

A prophetic heart pointed his finger at her, and it turned into a large sword with words inscribed on it: "Those who are hungry to know the truth will be willing to pay the price. They will turn aside from the destruction around them and turn to the Master with all their hearts. Hungry hearts will face the fires of the Master's refinery…and journey to the Third Mountain."

Restless and burning with fever, Hungry Heart tossed and turned on her small pallet and dreamed about the refinery. In her dreams she worked day and night to feed the hot fire, which refused to be satisfied. When the mercy hearts came and wiped her forehead with cool water, she lay more peacefully as her dreams immersed her in the soothing waters at the Master's Lagoon of Truth.

"Her wound is healing nicely," one mercy heart assured another. "She should wake soon and be able to hear the Master's voice. One word from him will make her strong again."

"Do you think we should try to wake her?" asked the second.

"No, she is still fighting something deep inside. The Master wants her heart to heal as well as her body," a third mercy heart responded as he looked to the Master for his approval. Still at Hungry Heart's side, the Master nodded in silent agreement.

Hungry Heart's dreams continued as she drifted in and out of sleep, waking only to take small sips of water and repeatedly ask, "Where am I? What happened? Where is the Master?" Although the mercy hearts tried to reassure her, the only voices she could hear came from deep within her dreams.

Searching Heart's voice cried out, "Run, run! The deceptive heart will find us and whip us if we do not work for him in the fields. Run, Hungry Heart, run!" The two of them ran through field after field, only to find themselves exhausted and facing the dreaded deceptive heart who had taken over the harvest field. Hungry Heart tried to find the Master, but every time she turned to look in a new direction, the deceptive heart stepped in front of her and commanded, "Work, or you will be sent to the Land of the Lost!"

"No!" she cried out fearfully in her sleep, so loudly that everyone in the cave glanced in her direction. The Master put his hand in hers and whispered quietly, "You do not have to be afraid, Hungry Heart. Face your fear and tell it to leave. You are not alone, nor have you ever been alone. The fear within you is not telling you the truth. Remember the paradigm of truth I gave you many years ago on the Plains of Hope? I am with you, even in the castle of your dreams."

Still dreaming, Hungry Heart clung to the Master's hand. She found herself on a narrow mountain path, slipping, losing her footing with each step, but the Master held her hand so tightly that her feet stepped lightly through the air itself. Then she was moving through room after room of an enormous castle, saying, "This castle reminds me of the paradigm I received from the Master." She looked down at the small golden paradigm in her hand, a tiny castle with five towers and a large open door.

"Your life is like a castle," the Master had taught her. "It has many rooms. I want to walk through each one of these rooms with you, but more than anything else, I want to sit in the throne room of your heart. Keep these rooms clean, Hungry Heart. Make room for me. I want to fill them with my love."

Her dream moved her down a long hallway with many doors until the ugly dragon stepped in front of her and threw its head back with a fiery snort. This time, without flinching, she stared into the green eyes and commanded firmly, "Go away! You cannot scare me; you do not belong here! Get out of this castle now! My heart belongs to the Master!" The dragon disappeared, and she stepped through the open door in front of her into a beautiful circular throne room with golden walls and a mirrored floor. The Master sat upon the golden throne with a translucent rainbow spread over his head and a large copy of the Great Book opened at his feet. His finger pointed to something printed on the page. She stepped closer and strained to see what it was...but before she could read the passage, she awoke.

Slowly, as the days passed, Hungry Heart grew stronger and stayed awake longer. One morning her eyes focused on the Master sitting quietly beside her. Shaking her head, her blocked ears opened, and she heard him singing a melody just for her.

So many roads to travel, so many mountains to climb.
So many sheep to shepherd, and vineyards to turn into wine.
The mountains are calling you onward, to go where your heart
   longs to go.
Rise and be healed, my daughter, the south wind is going to blow.
Promises are for my keeping, blessings are waiting for you,
No longer wounded and weary, paradigms always prove true.

He sang the little tune over and over again until Hungry Heart sat up on her own and finally stood to her feet. Taking small, shaky steps, she allowed him to lead her out through the cave entrance where they silently watched the chaotic, unauthorized siege still underway.

A few bold hearts poked the dragon with their swords while a band of strong hearts tried to bind its tail to the ground with ropes. Angry men and women shouted at each other, waving their swords in the air, and pushed, pulled, and scrambled for their next target. She shook her head with disgust, remembering her own participation in the battle.

"Master, why is this happening? Why did I join such a senseless assault?"

"It happens because there is no order. You wanted victory, but without my authority. I did not authorize this battle or your participation."

"Why do you allow it to continue?"

"Because it is their choice, just as it was yours."

Hungry Heart hung her head shamefully. "Please forgive me, Master. I did make a choice—the wrong one. I listened to the fear in my own heart and to the cries of men instead of your voice. I promise never to fight in battle again."

"Oh no, Hungry Heart, quite the contrary. You will fight, but you must learn to stand when you fight and to stand under my authority. The cries of men drove you to break rank. You were unable to hear me, and you became confused and thus put yourself in harm's way. Come, let's continue the journey, and I will teach you what you need to know. It's not going to be as difficult as you think.

"In fact," he smiled, "your heart has already learned what to do."

His words puzzled her again. Whatever did he mean? They stepped down from the cave entrance and continued south on the outermost edge of the fields to avoid the fighting. With each step Hungry Heart felt stronger, and the Master eventually challenged her to a short race through an orchard.

"Go ahead," he laughed. "I'll give you a head start. Let's see if you are willing to finish the race that is set before you!"

With all the strength she could muster, Hungry Heart took a deep breath and ran like the wind through the fruit trees. A flock of robins dove from the treetops and flew along beside her until she reached a large pond. To her surprise, the Master was there waiting for her, washing his feet in the cool water.

"I didn't see you pass me," she exclaimed in amazement. "Did you take a shortcut?"

"No," he chided playfully. "I'm just a bit swifter than you are. Besides,

I always go ahead of you to prepare the way, remember? Wasn't that one of the first paradigm pieces you received as a child?"

Blushing, she remembered the miniature gold path with footprints and the paradigm truth, "Never be afraid to follow me. I go before you always. I am before you, behind you, and beneath you. I am the path you walk upon and the sun that lights your way."

Ignoring her temporary lapse of memory, the Master invited her to join him at the water's edge. After she sat down, he tenderly removed one of her sandals and started to wash her foot.

"Oh, Master," she protested, "you don't need to do this. I can wash my own feet."

"Certainly you can, and you should at every opportunity. However, there may come a time when you need to wash someone else's feet, and I want you to know what a beautiful experience this is. Relax and let me take care of you."

Humbled by his words, Hungry Heart slipped off her other sandal and allowed him to wash her feet in the cool water and then gently wipe them with his own coat. After he finished, they picked some berries from the nearby bushes and headed out again.

"Master, I know that you want me to depend upon you one step at a time and that I should not try to live in tomorrow, but I smell something wonderful ahead. What is it?"

"That, Hungry Heart, is our next destination, the City of Bread. The aroma of bread fills this city day and night, and you will be invited to eat as much as you possibly can."

Just then a round-faced woman with bright red cheeks, sparkling dark eyes, and short curly red hair stepped onto the path with a friendly greeting.

"Hungry Heart, look what I have here for you—a basketful of sweet breakfast rolls. I know you must be hungry."

Hungry Heart glanced quickly at the Master as she reached for the basket. As her eyes met his gaze, she pulled back her hand.

"No, thank you, ma'am. I am on my way to the City of Bread with the Master, and I will wait."

"Wait? Nonsense. There is no need to wait. You are hungry now. Here, have one. The Master does not want you to be hungry."

The woman smiled again and held out the basket. Her white scalloped apron was so pretty against the folds of her long, bright yellow skirt. Hungry Heart suddenly blinked. This woman was not wearing the Master's blue coat of authority! Her clothing signaled an important warning. Everyone on the Second Mountain knew that any other form of clothing defied the Master's authority. From deep inside, Hungry Heart spoke firmly.

"No, I will wait for the Master's bread."

With that, the woman disappeared as suddenly as she had appeared.

"Master, who was that?" Hungry Heart quickly asked.

"That was the voice of temptation. You handled yourself quite well; you chose the better portion even though it meant that you might get hungry before we arrive. Did you notice how quickly she left when you spoke with firmness? See, you are learning how to wear your blue coat of authority with confidence."

The Master's encouragement made Hungry Heart smile, and they resumed walking. Hungry Heart thought about her experience as well as all the times in the past when she had given in to voices urging her to satisfy the immediate need. Normally she could be talked into almost anything because her hungry heart always wanted something. Today, however, she felt a bit stronger inside—more confident, more self-assured, and more focused on the Master instead of on her own desires.

Quite satisfied with herself and proud of the Master's approval, she failed to notice a dark-shadowed form lying stretched out across the road until she tripped over it.

Thump! The tip of a large, thick-scaled tail flipped up in the air and hit the ground again with enormous power before Hungry Heart had time to cry out. Aroused from its nap in the nearby bushes, the hideous creature swung its head around to see who had disturbed it, spitting fire from its long snout. It was the dragon, the feared creature from the Land of the Lost, which had been responsible for her experience in the battle!

The foul-smelling breath hit her face like hot steam and the pounding tail stirred up a thick dust cloud all around them. Frozen in her tracks, Hungry Heart waited for the Master to take charge. To her great surprise, he just stood there quietly, apparently unconcerned for their safety.

The dragon circled the pair slowly, never taking its shiny green eyes from theirs, slapping its tail against the ground and snorting enormous puffs of smoke. Its eyes dared them to fight back, to run, or even to cry out for help, but the Master refused to react. Trembling in fear, Hungry Heart quietly slipped as close to the Master's side as possible, put her hand in his and pleaded, "Master, do something."

"What did you just learn to do?"

"But that was a woman! A friendly, red-faced woman with a basket of bread. This is…this is…the…the…"

Hungry Heart could not even describe the hideous creature in front of them. Its ugliness defied any description she could think of. Just watching it circle them sent painful sensations through her head and made her knees weak.

"Tell it to leave," the Master replied matter-of-factly. "The dragon is here, but it is not wearing the blue coat of authority. Instead, it is covered with its own prideful ambition. You are the one wearing my authority. This is *my* mountain. Granted, it is free to roam and to entice you to fight or to run, but it is not free to violate my authority. Go ahead. Don't be afraid. Tell the creature to go away."

Hungry Heart tried to muster the courage to speak.

"Go away," she whispered, but her quivering voice only encouraged the beast to come closer.

"Go away," she said a bit louder, to no avail.

Then she noticed the green eyes watching her like an animal dueling for dominance and waiting for the slightest sign of intimidation. Instinctively, she fixed her gaze on the shiny green eyes that were challenging her. Hungry Heart refused to flinch. The longer she stared, the slower it moved, until it eventually stopped in its tracks and lowered its tail.

"That's it, Hungry Heart," the Master encouraged her with a hearty laugh. "You have discovered its weakness. You are the one here with authority. You are in control as long as you are standing here in my name. See there. The dragon is afraid of you! Now speak to it as if you were twice as tall and twice as fierce as it tries to be!"

Never taking her eyes from the predator's in front of her, Hungry Heart spoke firmly.

"Go away, you dirty thing. You do not scare me. This mountain belongs to the Master, and I belong to him! You can't do anything but try to make trouble. Go away—and go now!"

The mountains amplified her voice until it echoed from every direction like the noise of a mighty army. When it did, the creature's head spun around and, within moments, he disappeared into the trees.

"Well done, Hungry Heart," the Master cheered. "You are learning to stand as well as to walk in my authority. Never forget the lessons you have learned today. You are going to need them as your journey continues."

Hungry Heart did not understand at all, but the dragon was gone, and now she could smell the aroma of fresh-baked bread in the wind.

CHAPTER 15

The City of Bread

"Master," began Hungry Heart as they continued on their way, "you are the wisest heart of all. Where else can I possibly go to learn the things that I need to learn? I shudder to think where I would be now if you had not taught me how to stand up to the dragon and use your authority. The Second Mountain is a wonderful place indeed, and I want to learn everything you have to teach me here."

"That pleases me, Hungry Heart, but do you know what you are asking? Some truth is very difficult to receive."

"Oh, I am ready. I know I am. I have read and heard many hard sayings from the Great Book, as well as from others on this journey. Look, I have all these paradigm pieces of truth; there's so many that I can hardly count them anymore. I know that you love me and want only the very best for me. The Great Book says that you are the greatest teacher of all. Please, teach me everything."

"Everything? Well, that will take a very long time now, won't it," he teased her with a big grin. "The City of Bread is just up ahead. I think that will give you a good taste of my truth—and possibly another paradigm piece. First, though, you tell me. What do you already know about the bread of my bounty?"

"Well," began Hungry Heart, "I have often wondered why it is so dry and why the elders in the meeting places are so protective of it. One time I nearly choked on a very small piece, and Grandfather Humble Heart said that my heart was already too full. Now, how could that possibly be? I have a very hungry heart, don't I?"

Hungry Heart's question lingered in the air as they walked side by side in silence for a while. Even though the Master did not answer right away, a deep sense of contentment settled in her heart. She had asked, and he had listened. Her questions were important to him, just as she was.

"I promise to teach you about the bread of my bounty during our visit to the City of Bread," said the Master after a bit. "And in answer to your question, yes, you do have a hungry heart. Now I have a question for you. Are you hungry enough for the bread of my bounty?"

"Oh yes! I am very hungry, especially for your bread. I can smell it from here, and it is the most delightful fragrance in all the world."

In the distance, Hungry Heart could see the tall smokestacks reaching into the sky from the great bread ovens. As they drew closer to the city itself, they met ox-drawn wagons, loaded with wheat sheaves, en route to the Master's threshing floors and gristmills. There the grain would be ground into fine flour and carried to the stone kneading tables. Wagons, carts and even people on foot lined a second highway that left the city. They were laden with bundles of bread bound for the Plains of Hope, the Mountains of Faith, the Cities of Abiding Love, and even the Valley of Despair.

When they entered the city square, Hungry Heart expected to see a marketplace. Instead, piles of bread waited for hungry travelers on a long golden table. A wide gold crown molding surrounded the table's outer edge and prevented the large round loaves from falling off. Hungry Heart had never seen a table so beautiful or so long or filled so high with so much bread in all her life. Just the sight of it took her breath away.

"Oh my, I never, never, expected to see so much…" Hungry Heart's voice trailed off in awe.

Just as she was about to head toward the table, the Master pulled her down to sit with him on a bench in the square. He opened up his golden copy of the Great Book.

"Before we go any farther, you need to understand what bread is and what it is not," he explained. He read page after page about the bread of his bounty. When he closed the book, he quizzed her about baking bread.

"Hungry Heart, what do you know about baking bread?"

Hungry Heart tried to hide her exasperation. Everyone, even the smallest child in the Kingdom of Christianity, knew what bread was. Most of them also knew how to make it from flour, milk, water, honey, yeast and salt. Families mixed, kneaded, and baked these ingredients into every shape and description. Nearly everyone included bread in their daily diet. Why, she herself had learned to make bread at her mother's knee. They had mixed the dough in the large wooden bread bowl and took turns kneading it on the thick butcher-block tabletop. She loved the fragrance that filled their home on those days and the joy that fresh bread brought to the evening meal.

Now, it is true, she reasoned to herself, *the Master's bread is different. The elders speak about its unique composition, and they watch over it carefully when they divide it into very small portions during Celebration rituals.* Hungry Heart's experience included a wide variety of meeting places, and she had heard much discussion about exactly what this bread was and how it should be distributed. Many of the elders even argued and refused to visit one another's meeting places because of the bread. No, the Master's bread was no ordinary bread.

"My bread is life," the Master began to explain to her. "It is filled with every essential truth for life. Remember this: My bread is life, my life is truth, and my truth is the way that you must go in order to complete your paradigm quest. Here, on the Second Mountain, in the City of Bread, I prepare the bread of my bounty for all who seek it and who are willing to prepare their hearts to receive it. As long as men are satisfied with what they know, they do not search for what they do not know."

Hungry Heart nodded in agreement, but her thoughts drifted back to the Plains of Hope. Grandfather Humble Heart always made his bread very simply, using only a basic family recipe. He frowned at the fancy sweet breads sold in the village marketplace and warned Hungry Heart not to overindulge herself in them. "Healthy breads for healthy hearts," he used to say.

Just thinking about Grandfather Humble Heart gave her a moment of homesickness, and a tear slipped from her eye. Sometimes she almost expected to see her family at any moment. Other times, such as now, the separation hurt, and she longed for her homeland and family. As much as she loved the Master, she missed her parents, grandfather, aunts and uncles, cousins and friends—well, at least she missed most of her cousins.

There were a few, like Jealous Heart and Teasing Heart, whom she did not nor ever would miss. They had tormented and humiliated her in the most embarrassing ways all her life. Just the thought of their large mouths and nasty attitudes disgusted her.

More than one family member had warned them, "You change your hearts or you will find yourselves in the Land of the Lost one day. The Master is patient with you because you are children, but the day will come when you will be held accountable for your behavior. Your own hearts will deceive you, and the shadow creatures will carry you across the mountains on their wicked wings."

"The bread's miracle, you see," the Master continued seriously, interrupting her thoughts, "lies in your heart. The mystery belongs to me. It cannot be duplicated, replicated, or counterfeited successfully. It is the bread of my presence with you and the bread of fellowship with other hearts who love me. It is broken, pierced, and crushed to perfection. When you consume my truth, my life becomes a part of your heart in a very special way.

"The Great Refinery fires taught you to trust me with your life, and you learned to swim in my truth at the Lagoon of Truth. You received eyes to see and ears to hear in the Village of Enlightenment, and here you will receive an even deeper understanding of my truth—one that nourishes and satisfies the deepest needs of your heart."

Hungry Heart had difficulty separating the concept of natural breads, which she knew about, with the bread of his bounty, which was a mysterious link between the Master's life and hers. Again her thoughts wandered back to her parents' home and Grandfather's house on the Plains of Hope. There always had been plenty for her to eat—bread as well as fruits and vegetables—but her parents and Grandfather continually had encouraged her to eat the thin pieces of bread that could be found only at the meeting places. Wanting to please them, she did so. Still, for the most part, she found little pleasure in the dry bread and sometimes had difficulty swallowing it. She preferred the soft tasty sweet breads from the market or even Grandfather's hearty full-grain breads. Yet, here she was, sitting by the Master's side in the square of the City of Bread.

Just then, several street vendors passed by with their colorful bread carts and called out, "Fresh bread! Fresh bread! Tasty sweet breads for your journey!"

Looking forward to the bread on the golden table, she politely declined their offer and turned her attention back to the Master. After the vendors passed by, she followed the Master to the long golden table laden with large, flat, round bread cakes. A white powder covered the bread, looking like dusted flour. Hungry Heart's stomach rumbled in anticipation at the sight of this mysterious bread lying in the sun. However, she waited for her invitation to eat. In fact, she waited and waited. The Master did not reach for the bread, nor did he invite her to eat.

Other travelers mingled in the courtyard and surrounded the long ornate table. There were no chairs, yet its golden edging gave it a majestic ambiance, as if setting it aside for royalty and special invitation only. Tall golden goblets filled with sparkling dark red wines lined the very center from end to end. Some people, like herself, simply watched this mysterious table with excitement and anticipation. Religious hearts paraded in circles around it and read from the Great Book about the Master's bread. Repentant hearts knelt, loudly crying out their love for the Master. Joyful hearts sang songs, and servant hearts passed among the travelers to offer their assistance.

A small number, making eye contact with the Master and receiving his nod of approval, approached the table respectfully and accepted the bread cakes reverently from his hands. Hungry Heart waited anxiously for him to glance in her direction, but when he did he looked into her eyes and spoke words that pierced her heart.

"Hungry Heart, I know that you believe you are ready to eat. There is, however, more to partaking of this bread than simply eating it."

"More? But, Master, the bread will be dry and hard if I wait. I don't understand. Why can't I have it now while it is fresh and soft?"

The Master sighed deeply. Hungry Heart had come so far, yet she still had a long way to go. She had not yet learned to accept his truth without reason. Reason could be found anywhere for almost anything if one searched long enough; however, the assurance of things not seen could be found only deep in the heart. Patiently, he answered her question.

"The table is prepared for you, and you may eat as soon as your heart is prepared. Do you remember the pieces of bread you received in the meeting places, the ones that stuck in your throat?"

She bit her lip and acknowledged the awkward experiences he referred to. It had been quite embarrassing at the time.

"It does not matter whether you are here or back on the Plains of Hope—if your heart is not ready, you may not be able to swallow it. You must decide whether or not you want to go back to the street vendors to feed your hunger or wait here to prepare your heart. Walk through the city and talk with others, if you like. Take all the time you need."

Hungry Heart swallowed hard. What should she do? She glanced around at the crowd and saw a small group of fellow hungry hearts also watching the bread-filled tables in anticipation. She inched her way closer to the women in the group, but she still kept her eyes on the Master, expecting his eyes to invite her to eat at any moment.

A friendly heart also saw the gathering and greeted them with genuine kindness. His words sounded all too familiar to Hungry Heart, but his tone was warm. He tried to help everyone feel at ease.

"You know by now, my friends, that everyone's journey is unique and that it is not how far you go, but why you are going that makes the difference. My good friends, I am very interested to know why have you traveled this far?"

One by one, the hungry hearts answered him.

"I have come to taste this bread that I have heard so much about," a plump hungry heart answered quickly, as if in answering first he might receive his invitation to eat. His lips smacked with each word, and he never took his eyes off of the nearby table.

"I have come in the hope that I might receive my appointment from the Master to serve him here in this city. I have come from the Mountains of Faith, and I know that the bread of his bounty increases devotion and helps one to endure vigorous mountain life," another gentleman replied with great conviction.

A third man spoke up. "I have been eating sweet tasty breads all my life, and now look at me. I am short of breath and my heart is weak. I have come to find the bread that heals and strengthens instead of weakens. I have heard that miracles take place at this table."

Finally, the friendly heart turned to Hungry Heart and the other two women who had been standing by silently. "Now, ladies, why have you made this long journey? Don't be shy; we are all on this journey together."

"I do not know why I have come," the first answered meekly. "All I know is that I am here and more hungry to know the Master in new ways."

The other, a young mother with two small children at her side, confided, "I love the Master as well, but I have little time to think about a journey of my own these days. I have come because my husband insisted that I accompany him on his journey. He is over there with the religious hearts reading from the Great Book. So far, this journey has been long and difficult for me and the children, but I love my husband and will go where he wants me to go."

When it was her turn, Hungry Heart fumbled for just the right words. Finally they tumbled out of her mouth with a childlike innocence. "I am here because the Master has led me here. I am on my paradigm quest and headed for the Third Mountain to complete my paradigm and receive my appointment in the Master's service."

"Just listen to her," the plump man chided loud enough for everyone to hear. "She actually thinks she will reach the Third Mountain. She should be called a self-righteous heart instead of a hungry heart. Who among us believes that anyone dare approach the Master's throne and live to tell about it?"

Blushing, Hungry Heart turned away in humiliation. The friendly heart stopped her, "Wait, Hungry Heart. Don't let his words dissuade you from the call in your heart. Remember, you are following the Master, not the words of men."

Encouraged once again, Hungry Heart stood her ground and smiled thankfully at the friendly heart.

Just then one of the Master's assistants stepped to a platform near the golden table. Every voice stopped and every heart waited expectantly. Would this be an invitation to the table? Hungry Heart kept her eyes on the Master, who stood just behind his assistant.

"Welcome to the Master's City of Bread and to his table. You are free to travel anywhere in the city and to visit the threshing floors, the mills, the kneading stones, and even the great ovens. Water and fruit juices will be provided by the servant hearts, as well as a place for you to rest each night. You should, however, for your own sake, refrain from eating the Master's bread until your heart is prepared.

"Without this heart preparation, the bread of his bounty may make you ill. The Master's bread does not digest well if your heart is not in harmony with the Master and with one another. You will know, by the Master's eyes, when you are ready to approach the golden table.

"You are also free to approach the street vendors for bread. Their bread will satisfy immediate needs, if necessary, until your heart preparation is complete. The choice, as always, is yours. Enjoy your stay in the City of Bread and do not hesitate to ask for assistance if necessary."

Two of the hungry-hearted men spoke quietly with each other before inching their way closer to the table. The young mother left the group to find out what her husband wanted to do. The other two hungry hearts decided to join a nearby group of joyful hearts to sing about the bread until the Master granted his approval, while a few anxious hearts dashed out for the bread vendors. Hungry Heart looked around for the Master and saw him watching her from the distance, but his eyes did not invite her to the table.

Bewildered, she wandered through the city. Regardless of where she went, she could not escape the call of the street vendors offering their fresh bread.

"Come, eat, and be satisfied! Bread from the Second Mountain waits for you! Begin each day with bread that satisfies! Come, be filled, and rejoice! The Master is a gracious host and does not want you to be hungry!"

One by one, restless and impatient hearts gave up and stepped up to the vending carts to accept the fresh, tasty, and available bread. The blue-robed vendors passed out their bread, read from the Great Book, and encouraged the travelers to come back for more from their wagons. Many travelers decided to join the vendors or to become vendors themselves when they saw how fulfilling the work was. After all, the Great Book did say, "Feed the hungry."

"Makes you want some real bad, doesn't it?" a voice spoke up behind Hungry Heart. She turned to see a faithful heart watching the scene with her. "But don't give in, Hungry Heart. The vendors have good hearts; they love the Master and want to help, but they prepare their bread quickly and try to convince everyone that their particular portion is special. There is a danger in becoming dependent upon the vendor's carts instead of the Master's table. You hang in there—you'll be glad you did. The Master has prepared the bread that you need for your journey, and it will not fail you. Be patient and prepare your heart. It will be worth it. You'll see."

"But I am so confused. Please tell me, what am I supposed to do to prepare my heart?"

"No one can show you the depths of your heart and the impurities that need to be swept away but the Master himself—keep your eyes on him." Before she could ask anything else, the faithful heart disappeared down the crowded street.

Four days passed. Hungry Heart's legs grew weak and her stomach hurt. She had traveled from one end of the city to the other and spent endless hours waiting by the golden table. Every day she had stood there and watched the assistants sprinkle a white powder on the bread.

Every day the Master had continued to encourage her, as did other travelers, but each time she approached him for permission to eat, his eyes penetrated her heart and she turned away. He could see something that did not belong there, but what was it?

A servant heart had found her a place to lie down to rest in a secluded house away from the fights that had started to break out among a few overbearing zealous hearts. Out in the streets, angry hearts lashed out at one another and suspicious hearts accused each other of sneaking bread from the Master's table unfairly. At the end of each day, very hungry and somewhat anxious herself, Hungry Heart buried her head in the pillow and cried herself to sleep. Yet another day had passed, and she had failed to please the Master's penetrating eyes. The worst part was, she did not know what she was supposed to do!

The next day, she joined a group of religious hearts and listened to them read from the Great Book about the Master's bread. It was, the Great Book said, the only way to receive lasting satisfaction in his service. The ingredients could not be duplicated anywhere. He prepared his truth with great sacrificial love and offered it as bread. Consuming the bread of his bounty meant that one consumed his truth and love in a very tangible way.

On the sixth day, she moved weakly to the golden table and stood there like a hungry street urchin watching others feast. By mid-afternoon, underneath the hot sun, a group of bitter hearts pushed their way through the crowd and demanded, "We have waited long enough! We deserve to be fed; life has been unfair so far. We do not have to face unfairness here at the Master's table."

Stunned, Hungry Heart watched them lunge for the table, gather handfuls of bread and devour it as quickly as possible. The Master watched them silently. Within moments they started to choke and gag, one after another, spitting and coughing up pieces of bread until they fell to their knees and cried out for the Master's mercy. With that, a troop of mercy hearts helped them to limp away from the table and took them down a side street.

Hungry Heart leaned weakly against a nearby wall while the Master's assistants sprinkled the white powder on the bread. She strained to remember what it was called. Somewhere, someone had mentioned this white powder. Was it sweet? Did it make the bread soft? She could not remember. Understanding her confusion, the Master stepped up beside her and answered her unspoken question.

"That, Hungry Heart, is the dust of long-suffering. It preserves my truth and love in a very special way and is bittersweet to the taste."

"S-s-suf-fering..." she stammered. "How can you possibly ask me to eat bread that has been sprinkled with suffering? Haven't I suffered enough? The journey has been so long and so difficult, and now I am almost too weak to speak. I will need someone to help me to the table if I endure until tomorrow... And you want me to eat suffering...bittersweet suffering?"

"The choice, as always, is yours, Hungry Heart. However, consider this before you decide. It is far better to share my suffering than to endure your own. I will be with you and keep you in my love forever as long as you share my life. Your concept of suffering and patient endurance will be transformed as you partake of my bread. Today you see it as pain. Tomorrow you will count it all joy. The mystery, my daughter, is at the table. It can be measured only as you share in my suffering and feast on the bread of bounty."

Too weak to question him any longer, Hungry Heart just shook her head. She didn't understand, and she stopped asking for permission to eat. Bread? Love? Suffering? Mystery? What did it all mean, anyway? She even stopped asking questions. Her heart felt empty, as if purged from the ability to reason, much less to decipher a riddle. Interestingly enough, after her questions ceased, the physical hunger pangs subsided and the desperation in her heart gave way to peace once again.

Something else odd occurred at the same time. She could not stop thinking about her cousins, Jealous Heart and Teasing Heart. She kept seeing their faces in her mind's eye and hearing their voices taunting her. For the first time in many years, the memories did not hold her in the grip of bitterness and resentment. Rather, she started to remember the countless times that she had offended or hurt someone with her own words and behaviors, knowingly and unknowingly.

She pondered the Master's love for her, her cousins and those whom she, too, had treated unfairly over the years. He had given so much love for everyone. How could she possibly withhold hers? A single tear slipped from her eyes as she fell asleep that night. It had not been easy to recognize this empty place buried deep in her heart; but, as she did, the ache in her heart disappeared.

"Hungry Heart, wake up! The seventh day has arrived. The Master is waiting for you," an assistant's words stirred her out of a deep sleep, and he helped her to her feet. Still groggy, she slowly stepped out into the courtyard and up to the golden table. Many other travelers were present as well, but Hungry Heart saw only one person: the Master. He looked beautiful, radiant and so pleased to see her there. His eyes invited her to approach the table. In one hand he held the precious bread she had waited so long to receive, and in the other hand he held a golden cup filled with a delicate fruit of the vine.

CHAPTER 16

The Master Speaks in New Ways

————•+•————

Neither the bread's texture nor its taste commanded Hungry Heart's attention. For a brief span of time, her natural senses stood quiet as she fed upon the nature and substance of life itself. Lifting one of the golden cups to her lips, the Master smiled and invited her to drink.

After the meal, she fell to her knees and wept.

"Master, you are the bread of my life. Although I did not deserve to even hold out my hand, you have fed me from your table. Your love is gracious and merciful, far more than I ever dared to imagine. Your truth reaches into the innermost parts of my being and calls me to find my satisfaction in you and you alone. Your truth is pulsating through my heart and calling me to draw still closer to you. I do not know how it will be possible; these things are far beyond my understanding, yet I am willing."

She lifted her arms in the air, surrendering her life as completely as she possibly could. At that moment, enraptured in the beauty of his presence, she felt as though she could follow him anywhere.

Accepting her tribute with a smile, the Master placed a new symbolic piece in her right hand—a golden cup with a sheaf of wheat on one side and a cluster of sparkling grapes on the other side.

"Oh, Master, it is beautiful! I will treasure it forever, and I will tell the story of your table again and again at every opportunity."

Her awe gave way to the exuberant joy and spirit of celebration in the city square. Spontaneously, hearts of every description joined in song about the Master's wonderful feast. A dancing heart grabbed Hungry Heart by the hand and pulled her into a dance around the table. She clapped her hands and laughed with delight until she fell down near the foot of the golden table, exclaiming in wonder, "I have tasted the bread of life, and it has changed my heart. The Master's life is in the bread, and the bread is in the Great Book! He has given us every word to feed upon. How great is his name! Blessed be the Master of our hearts!"

The celebration continued for days. Travelers came, prepared their hearts and received their invitation to the table. Some, too eager to prepare, turned to the bread vendors for an immediate satisfaction. At first it was almost impossible to tell the difference between those who feasted at the Master's table and those who depended upon the vendors for bread. Everyone appeared joyful and thankful just to be in the City of Bread.

Eventually, subtle distinctions did surface. The hearts who followed the Master's instructions to "wait and prepare your heart" appeared to be stronger and healthier. The bread from the vendors' carts produced joy, yet it did not endure. They had to keep returning to the vendors, requiring more and more bread to reach the same level of contentment. Many started to gain an unseemly amount of weight and required new blue robes. If they did not remain faithful to a specific vendor, the different bread from other vendors often didn't digest as well.

On the other hand, one small crumb from the Master's table sustained Hungry Heart for a very long time. Oh, the Master offered her as much as she could possibly eat, but it did not take very much to satisfy her hunger, sharpen her mind, and strengthen her body.

From time to time she caught the Master's eye looking into her heart, and she retreated to a quiet place to discover whatever it was that should not be there. The smallest offense against anyone, intentional or not, needed to be emptied from her heart before he would invite her back to his table again. She cooperated, willingly and joyfully, because now she knew the benefits of the bread in her life. Never had she felt so free, so satisfied, and so joyful.

Sometimes others remarked about the changes taking place within her. More than one traveler commented, "I do believe that the Master is getting ready to give you a new name. Your eyes are different—you just don't look like a hungry heart any longer."

Nevertheless, the Master continued to address her as "Hungry Heart," because he could still see and hear the deep hungers inside her. She yearned to reach the Third Mountain and complete her paradigm quest. The hunger for her appointment in his service grew stronger with each passing day. As much as she loved the City of Bread, she finally requested, "Master, is it time to continue my journey yet? I feel so much stronger now and ready to travel to the Third Mountain. I see others moving on, and I want to go as well."

After he gave her request sufficient consideration, he decided, "I want you to spend some more time here, at my table, and with the other travelers."

"With the other travelers?" Hungry Heart asked, puzzled. "You told me long ago that I did not need traveling companions and that I should keep my eyes on you. You are all that I need. Every time I take my eyes from you, I find myself in all sorts of trouble."

"You have learned that lesson well," he laughed. "The truth of the matter has not changed. You must keep your eyes on me. However, now it is time for you to learn to see me and hear me in many other ways. Look at the travelers who are feasting on the bread of my bounty. You all eat from the same table; therefore, you all have the same truth inside you."

In spite of his past reprimands not to be concerned with the failures and weaknesses of others, she could not resist asking, "But what about those who eat from the vendor carts? What kind of truth do they have inside them? Oh, Master, it would be very harmful indeed for me to listen to those who have refused to prepare their hearts for your table—and sometimes it is difficult to tell the difference."

"Hungry Heart, listen closely and hold these words in your heart. You will not understand them now, but before you leave this city you will. The bread vendors are here because I have asked them to serve me here. It is true that they are overzealous at times. It also is true that their bread contains ingredients that I do not permit at my table. Yet it is not up to you to judge the vendors or the travelers.

"Now, I want you to mingle with everyone. Greet, meet and fellowship with others. Talk to the bread vendors and listen to their hearts. Share paradigm stories and read the Great Book together. As you do this, watch for me in their eyes and listen for me in their voices. Learn to distinguish my truth from the words of man."

With that he turned into the crowd and disappeared from sight. Hungry Heart ran after him, calling, "Wait! Wait for me, Master. I cannot find you."

"Oh, for goodness' sakes, stop that crying," a short, disgruntled heart rebuked her. "Do you think you are the only one here with a problem? I have more troubles than you ever have thought about having. I've just learned that my entire family has moved down to the Valley of Despair because I've been gone so long, and the shadow creatures surround their house day and night with tormenting threats. My wife is ill, and the children think I have deserted them. Here, take this hankie. Get yourself together or you'll end up in the Pity House with the self-pity hearts. Then you really will have problems."

"I can't find the Master," Hungry Heart cried. "I don't know where to find him, and the streets are so crowded here."

"Well, until you take your eyes off yourself, you never will find him," he retorted, then hustled off to send a messenger with an encouraging word for his family.

After dismissing his disgruntled insights and deciding that he had eaten too much from the vendors, Hungry Heart wandered through the city wiping her eyes and asking everyone she met, "Have you seen the Master pass this way?"

Helpful hearts pointed her in various directions. Religious hearts read to her from the Great Book, while pious hearts agreed to call him for her. A small group of studious hearts had a new suggestion.

"Why don't you enroll in the Master's school? The best teachers in the city should be able to help you find the Master. It's over there, in that large round building called 'The Place of His Hearts'."

Filled with hope, Hungry Heart headed for the school. Inside, hearts of every description gathered together in small, mixed groups. Up until this point, like hearts had attracted like hearts, sharing their common interests and benefiting from their similarities on their journeys. Here, no one seemed to care about distinctive personalities, heart qualities or homelands. Only one concern was paramount: learning to see and hear the Master with an open heart.

The school officials welcomed Hungry Heart and immediately enrolled her in her first study group, where everyone talked about themselves, their families, and their journeys. They shared paradigm pieces and referred to lessons from the Great Book. Much to Hungry Heart's surprise, the group leader, Delightful Heart, was one of the bread vendors. He had traveled to the City of Bread many years ago and eaten at the golden table. He knew the benefits of heart preparation and the healing qualities to be found there.

In fact, he still made regular visits to the golden table and fellowshipped with the Master at every opportunity.

"Why then," Hungry Heart asked pointedly and with a note of criticism in her voice, "do you prepare an inferior bread, which only weakens people and creates a dependency on you? Why don't you send the travelers to the Master's golden table for the bread of his bounty?"

Instead of taking offense at her words, Delightful Heart reached for his completed paradigm to explain his appointment in the Master's service.

"Oh," Hungry Heart exclaimed in surprise as soon as she saw it, "you have your paradigm and your appointment—here as a vendor! It is very beautiful indeed! Please forgive my critical heart and tell me your paradigm story."

The group crowded in to see Delightful Heart's paradigm. Very graciously he allowed everyone to touch the round gold locket hanging securely from a chain around his neck. One continuous, smooth, golden line formed a spiral pattern on it that created three circles embedded with blue sapphires and white diamonds. At the very center of the gem-studded golden spiral was a large, star-shaped ruby. Ever so carefully he opened the locket to reveal one small crumb from the Master's table.

"I began my paradigm quest with a desire to travel as far as the Third Mountain, just like you, Hungry Heart. However, once I arrived at this city I could not stop hearing the cries of hungry people wandering through the streets day after day, either unable to find their way to the golden table or too eager to wait. I pleaded with the Master to have mercy upon them.

"One day, he found me kneeling at the golden table unable to eat because of their cries. How could I have so much when they had so little? There, in answer to my question, he asked me to prepare as much bread as I possibly could and to feed the hungry to the best of my ability with this paradigm truth: 'My people are perishing because they are hungry. Feed them until wisdom opens their eyes and they are able to receive the bread of my bounty.'"

Delightful Heart pointed to his paradigm to explain. "These three circles represent his dwelling place, each one moving closer to the center where the red fire of his presence burns on the Third Mountain. The blue and white gemstones speak of heaven and earth moving together in perfect harmony to create a pathway for travelers. The pathway itself is unbroken, but there are separations or stepping stones between heaven and earth.

Many travelers are able to move from one dimension to the next and their journey moves quickly. Others continue just so far until they, for many reasons, are unable to step into the next realm of discovery. Moving from the bread that man prepares to the Master's table is one such step."

Indeed, Delightful Heart had sacrificed the desires of his own heart for the Master by serving others here in the City of Bread. In the same way, Loving Heart and Sacrificial Heart had been there for Hungry Heart when she needed them. After Hungry Heart realized this, she looked into Delightful Heart's eyes and saw something else. She saw the Master's love!

Another member of the group spoke up. "I served the Master for many years as an elder in the City of Abiding Love. My friends and I started many schools and study circles like this one. We encouraged ambitious social endeavors to help the needy hearts and to reach out to the homeless. People came from the far corners of the kingdom of Christianity to hear us speak about the Master's love. One day I looked into my own heart and knew that I had to find the source of his love. My journey led me here, to the City of Bread, and I have been here ever since. I am still discovering what it means to abide in his love. The more I learn, the more I realize how little I really know."

"What have you learned? Please tell me," Hungry Heart urged him. She remembered the beautiful transformation in Loving Heart's life, and she heard the same soft-spoken compassion coming from this man. As much as she loved the Master and her family and friends back home, Hungry Heart did not actually love her fellow travelers. Her attempts to be courteous and kind sometimes barely sufficed as polite—and often failed completely.

"The Master loves us enough to give himself completely to each and every one of us and our needs, regardless of our ability to love him in return. He gives without expectations and receives our devotions with true humility. We should be like him in every way possible, especially in love for one another. Loving someone else is not as difficult as it seems, if we allow the Master's life to live in us. We can be his hands, his feet, his eyes, and his voice for each other."

Hungry Heart listened intently. This man spoke with such authority, conviction and purpose—yet with such compassion. His voice sounded like the Master's. Suddenly, it all started to make sense.

Hungry Heart wasn't alone after all; the Master had not deserted her in the City of Bread. She did have her eyes on the Master and her ears tuned to his voice. At that moment, her heart opened to an entirely new dimension of understanding. The Master's truth lived in these fellow travelers just as it lived in her. *Oh my,* she lamented silently. *How often did I fail to hear him back on the Plains of Hope?*

The group read from the Great Book late into the night. This time, instead of hearing "about" the Master, she listened for him in every word. Paradigm stories flew back and forth from one open heart to another. Everyone's personal experience with the Master became an impartation of life for the entire group.

"Hungry Heart, I have a word for you. I believe that you are prepared to hear it now," a strong voice announced from behind her. She turned around to see a prophetic heart, the same one who had spoken under the almond tree after the North Wind. She had never forgotten his words: "The Master has sent the North Wind to blow away everything that has not been rooted and grounded in him...your hearts have become self-sufficient. Blessed be the Master for sending the North Wind."

Speechless and trembling, Hungry Heart waited for the prophetic heart to approach her. He put one hand on her shoulder and raised the other in the air as he spoke loudly enough for everyone to hear.

"Hungry Heart, you have traveled a great distance and learned a great many things at the Master's feet. You have been satisfied and filled beyond your dreams, yet you are still hungry for more—and more is what the Master has for you. He will give you more and more until you cry out for him to stop."

The air itself grew heavy with the weight of his words and pressed upon her until she fell to the ground. Prophetic Heart continued to speak with great boldness, and her heart reached up to receive his message.

"He will take you so far that you will never be able to go back, yet in going forward you will find yourself going back. The beginning is the end and the end is the beginning. There is a time of deep darkness approaching, but the Master says to you, 'Be not afraid, for in the darkness you will learn to walk with eyes and ears of faith.' You will cry out for understanding, but it will not come. You will cry out for him, and he will be there. Blessed be the Master! He has sent the North Wind, but the South Wind will blow soon and the fruit of your life will grow in abundance."

He finished speaking and walked away, leaving Hungry Heart lying on the ground under the awesome presence of the Master's words—words that both confirmed and confused her, strengthened and stretched her. Still unable to move, she submitted to the soft waves of incredible peace flooding through her body while the rest of the group sang soft songs of love and adoration for the Master.

CHAPTER 17

The Royal Highway

The Master's school gave Hungry Heart the opportunity to carefully research her new pieces in the Great Book. She learned the art of discussion, debate, and positive dialogue. In the process she realized that her confrontation long ago at the Lagoon of Truth with the serious heart over whether or not the Master laughed might have resulted in a good discussion instead of a "win or lose" battle of words.

In addition to her schoolwork, Hungry Heart was busy with the city's activities, especially the daily celebrations at the golden table. No one ever knew exactly what the Master planned for any given day, but this only added to everyone's anticipation and expectation. The music could be upbeat or very quiet. Prophetic hearts would move freely among the travelers and bestow verbal encouragement. Perhaps the most exciting moments of all were when weak and ill travelers tasted the Master's bread and received healing miracles! One day Hungry Heart witnessed a lame woman toss away her cane and actually join the dance!

Every so often a swarm of nasty, winged spirit creatures tried to infiltrate the city. No one paid much attention to them, however, and the sounds of music drove them away instantly. All in all, the City of Bread proved to be an amazing place, filled with the aroma of fresh bread, good fellowship and, above all, the Master's truth.

As everyone studied paradigm truth and read from the Great Book, Hungry Heart could see the Master in their eyes and hear him in their voices. She often caught a glimpse of his familiar figure smiling at her from a distance, and every so often she could hear the sound of his voice in the wind. However, her dependency upon a solitary experience with him lessened, and she learned to appreciate the wide variety of ways he wanted to speak to her.

Although content and happy in the City of Bread, Hungry Heart still longed to complete her paradigm quest. Sometimes at night she climbed to the highest tower in the city and tried to catch a glimpse of the Third Mountain, but the smoky cloud beyond the Second Mountain prevented her from seeing anything really clearly.

One morning, a group of her classmates spotted her at the golden table eating the bread of his bounty and cried out, "There you are, Hungry Heart! We've been looking all over the city for you. Listen! Do you hear that music coming from the east? Isn't it beautiful? Hurry, let's go see where it's coming from!"

"Now? You want to leave now? We may miss the Celebration if we go now... ."

"The Great Book says," Precocious Heart proclaimed, "that today is the day. Do not worry about tomorrow and concentrate on today. Besides, can't you hear it? The Master's voice is singing, and I have never heard him singing with such devotion. How can we not go? I do believe he is calling us, don't you, Hungry Heart?"

Hungry Heart listened closely and, sure enough, far away and to the east she could hear the Master's voice singing. With her bread in hand she joined her friends. What a sight they made! Like a flock of blue geese, they scurried as fast as they could in their long blue linen coats, chattering and straining their necks to find the source of the music. Naturally, a few curious hearts joined them, and before long a band of joyful hearts came along as well.

When they reached the city's border they found some devoted heart musicians packing their instruments in large wagons. A few bread vendors waited to travel with them.

"Devoted hearts, where are you going?" Hungry Heart inquired politely.

"We are going to join the Master's chorus on the far side of this mountain. Don't you hear him singing? He is calling us to come to his Gardens of Devotion to sing for him. It is a great honor, indeed. So now we're headed to the Royal Highway, which will lead us to the gardens."

"Oh my," replied Hungry Heart, "we heard the music, too, and it's so beautiful that we want to follow it. May we join you?"

The devoted heart who appeared to be the leader of the group did not share her enthusiasm. "I'm not quite certain how appropriate that would be. Do any of you sing? Do you play instruments? Do you participate in the Master's great devotional dramas?" he fired off one question after another.

Two ambitious hearts started expounding on their past experiences, while a family of insecure hearts turned back, shaking their heads in disappointment.

Hungry Heart tried diplomacy. "If you allow us to accompany you, we promise to follow behind you and not hinder your journey. Perhaps you may even be able to share your paradigms of devotional truth with us, and we know that will please the Master."

"All right," the devoted heart conceded, "you may come, but you must cease all this chatter immediately. Devotion requires silence. Unless we still our own hearts and mouths, we won't be able to concentrate on the Master's singing and might lose our way. This is our first time to come this way, and we have heard that the Royal Highway is still under construction in many places. Do you absolutely promise to follow behind us, to be very quiet, and to respect our meditations?" he asked very sternly.

"Oh yes, we will!" The group cheered loudly before everyone immediately clapped their hands over their mouths at Devoted Heart's disapproving glance. The cheers settled down to quiet whispers and then to silence before Devoted Heart gave his final approval. Then he signaled for the wagons to move out as he stepped forward on the Royal Highway to lead the quiet, reverent processional to the Gardens of Devotion. The only sound that could be heard came from the tinkling bells on their blue coats and the hint of music in the wind ahead of them.

Devoted hearts were not known for their people-friendly personalities. They usually spent the majority of their time in seclusion with the Master or with each other in quiet solitude. No one challenged their love for the Master and the Great Book, but they were very difficult to understand and relate to.

Without the opportunity to talk or ask questions, Hungry Heart focused on the beautiful landscape and the wide, spacious Royal Highway. The majority of her journey had not been easy. This road was a pleasure in comparison to the long dark catacombs leading to the Great Refinery, the trail to the Lagoon of Truth, and the tedious descent to the foot of the Second Mountain. She shuddered as she remembered her narrow escape with

Searching Heart from the harvest fields. And her journey from the Village of Enlightenment had been fraught with danger! The Master could go anywhere in a moment of time, yet he always seemed to lead her on the longest and most difficult route, assuring her that it added strength to the strength already in her life.

Here, on the Royal Highway, every high place had been made low and every low place had been raised so that it was easy even for the eldest among them to travel. Flowering shrubs and fruit trees lined the roadway. Every few miles, giant shade trees and clear streams provided peaceful places to rest. At each rest stop, the devoted hearts gathered together for their meditations. In consideration, they always left a small opening in their circle for others to join them, and from time to time a few did. However, the majority of Hungry Heart's friends and new companions waited patiently in the distance and whispered with excited anticipation about the Master's gardens. They opened up their copies of the Great Book and learned as much as they could about their destination.

"It says here," reported Seeking Heart, "that the Master planted his gardens to provide a place for true devotion and meaningful meditation. It also says that he burns incense there, a fire that transforms our devotions into acceptable offerings before they rise to the heavens."

Hungry Heart leaned forward with a note of caution in her voice. "A fire? What kind of fire?"

"I don't know. It just says here that he does not allow strange fire to burn in his garden."

Instinctively, they all turned their heads to look in the direction of the devoted hearts. Seeking Heart questioned aloud, "Perhaps only the devoted hearts will be allowed to enter this garden? Perhaps our journey will be in vain?" No one answered.

The bread vendors moved among the group quietly distributing bread to anyone who wanted it. No longer able to shout and advertise their wares, they quietly acknowledged hungry looks and then moved on. Instead of asking for their bread, Hungry Heart reached into her coat and pulled out the chunk of bread from the golden table that she had not taken time to eat. Not knowing how long the journey might be, she pulled off a small piece and then put the rest back in her pocket. When she looked up, it was to find the others watching her.

In the City of Bread, only the Master gave the invitation to approach his table and eat the bread of his bounty. Hungry Heart looked back at the group. Did she dare share her portion with others? Were their hearts prepared to receive it? Back on the Plains of Hope, the elders distributed the bread of his bounty at the meeting places. So, apparently the Master did make provision for times like this, but was this one of those times? Her companions understood her dilemma and stood back quietly, allowing her the freedom to decide what to do.

She closed her eyes and tried very hard to listen to the Master's voice in her heart, just as she had been learning to do at school. After a few moments, the anxiety passed and a peaceful presence surrounded her. She knew that the Master was close at hand even though she could not see him, and she knew what to do.

Looking straight into the eyes of those who stood waiting, she spoke with the Master's authority. "You know how important it is that your hearts be prepared to receive the bread of his bounty. Prepare your hearts, listen for his invitation, and then we will eat together."

They nodded silently and bowed their heads. Even the bread vendors slipped into the circle. One by one, they extended their hands for the bread of his bounty, and she broke off a small portion for each one.

By sundown the travelers could see bright lights in the distance and hear the music very clearly. Forgetting their pious postures, the devoted hearts broke into a run and darted down the Royal Highway with shouts of thanksgiving to the Master for safely leading them to the gardens.

Hungry Heart and her companions followed at a respectful distance until they reached the end of the highway. Standing on a hilltop overlooking the Gardens of Devotion, they saw trees, flowers, and gentle streams dot the landscape. A sea of people moved in and out of large open-air amphitheaters. From their position, the group could see dozens of theater stages and wide platforms facing east with great seating areas in front of the stages and tall torches lighting the aisles. Musicians and large choirs performed on the stages. Some music sounded incredibly beautiful while other sounds hardly resembled music at all.

"What is this?" Joyful Heart asked excitedly, then answered her own question. "This is wonderful! Everyone is singing the Master's praise and performing just for him. Look! They're dancing! Oh, I must go down there as quickly as I can. Please forgive me for not waiting for the rest of you, but I must join in the dance! I have waited so long for this!"

With that, she sprinted down to the nearest theater and disappeared into a maze of bodies moving in rhythm to the music.

"I am not certain about this," Doubtful Heart murmured loud enough for everyone in the group to hear. "I don't see where the devoted hearts went, and I can't hear the Master's song in the wind any longer."

"How can anyone hear anything?" Serious Heart retorted. "There must be something wrong here. This is much too loud and confusing. The Great Book says to avoid confusion. I'm not sure about this place..."

"Welcome to the Master's Gardens of Devotion," a faithful heart greeted the group and spoke up clearly. "Come and join us. The gardens may not be exactly what you expected to find, but they are filled with variety, aren't they? And here," waving her hand over the valley, "the Master has planted every variety of devotion imaginable. Everyone will be able to find the garden spot of his or her choice. You also will be able to practice many forms of devotion to the Master."

Serious Heart shook his head and snapped at her, "Well, I am not going anywhere but back to the City of Bread. I didn't put up with this foolishness back in the old meeting places on the plains, and I'm not going to put up with it here. Devotion requires order and reverence. This looks like a circus for children. I will give my devotion to the Master at the golden table, where it belongs." With that, he thumped his copy of the Great Book against his knee and turned back. Several others agreed and followed him.

A young hopeful heart looked around apprehensively. She had waited for such a long time to learn the truth about devotion and had received several paradigm pieces encouraging her to increase her devotion to the Master, but this was so far from what she expected.

"Perhaps," she asked the faithful heart, "there are other Gardens of Devotion on the Second Mountain?"

"No. I have served the Master in the Great Devotional Dramas here for many years, and I have never heard of or been to other gardens. This is it, just as you see it before you. This is the place where travelers come to express their love, adoration and thanksgiving to the Master. As you can see, it stands at the very foot of the Second Mountain. There is no place to go from here except to the Third Mountain, and only a very few hearts choose to go there. Come with me, and I will take you to the visitor's center. From there you can decide which gathering to attend. You may even want to start one of your own. The garden is very large; there's always room for new songs and new expressions of devotion."

The majority of the group headed down the hill with the smiling faithful heart. Hungry Heart, Hopeful Heart, and Trusting Heart stayed behind.

"Just maybe," a very old woman suggested as she passed by, "you young folks need to find a wisdom heart. There's one down there, you know, just past the choir of pious hearts, in the Garden of Contemplation." The three young hearts were startled at the old woman's unexpected presence, but she just kept moving, as if every moment counted.

Now they had to make a decision. They could go back or go ahead because it seemed rather senseless to stay where they were, so the three decided to go down to look for the wisdom heart the old woman had spoken about. Hungry Heart inquired again and again of people they passed, but no one seemed to know where he was, much less where the Garden of Contemplation was.

Everyone knew about the Garden of Rejoicing, and more than one traveler warned them to stay away from the Garden of Enthusiastic Rockers unless they had earplugs. There were gardens filled with old songs from the meeting places and gardens filled with new songs. One place seemed particularly unusual—everyone was singing in a different language.

"That," one of the hearts standing nearby informed them, "is the Garden of Unknown Tongues. Why anyone wants to speak and sing in a language he can't understand is beyond me. If I am going to give the Master anything, I certainly intend to know what I am saying to him."

Hungry Heart could not resist the temptation to stop for a peek. She found hundreds of hearts on their knees, singing the same melody in different languages. It isn't all that bad, she decided. In fact, it sounded quite beautiful. She considered staying, but they needed to find the wisdom heart as soon as possible, so she quietly excused herself and returned to the search.

Finally, deep in the heart of the gardens, they found a small inconspicuous garden surrounded by fragrant white gardenia bushes. A little wooden sign on the gate read, "The Garden of Contemplation." The very moment they stepped past the gate, every sound ceased—except for a sweet gentle song coming from a small blue bird in the tree above them.

Hungry Heart blinked in disbelief. There, rocking back and forth to the rhythm of the bird's song, in an old wicker rocking chair, was Wisdom Heart—the very same wisdom heart she had met at the base of the First

Mountain. He had told her that storms followed her wherever she went because of the chaos in her life. He recognized her immediately.

"Hungry Heart, just look at you! I see that you have come a long way; yet, I believe you have a long way to go. But you are here now, and that is the important thing. It is good to see the sun shining around you," he added with a twinkle in his eye. "What brings you here, to this insignificant place in the Gardens of Devotion? Surely you young folks would much rather be out where things are, as they say, 'happening.' I understand they even jump up and down for the Master in some gardens." He chuckled quietly. "The older I get, the more ways I find to offer my devotion right here in my good ole rocking chair. I guess you could say I'm a'rockin' for the Master, Hungry Heart."

"Wisdom Heart, these are my companions, Trusting Heart and Hopeful Heart. They have traveled with me since the City of Bread. We have listened to the Master together, but now we are uncertain about where to go or what to do. An old woman sent us to you. Can you help us?"

Wisdom Heart leaned back in his chair and watched the little bird in the tree above them before he spoke.

"That little bird knows how to sing for the Master. It knows which song to sing and when to sing. It knows where its nest is and where danger is."

The blue bird continued to sing, while Wisdom Heart continued to rock and Hopeful Heart shifted from foot to foot nervously.

Unable to hold back the words rising up in her throat, Hopeful Heart burst out, "Wisdom Heart, you are very wise, and we are very honored to be here with you. We do want to sing like the bird, but there is something we want even more."

"And what might that be?" Wisdom Heart smiled knowingly.

"To give the Master our devotion here in these beautiful gardens."

Wisdom Heart stood up and looked directly into Hopeful Heart's eyes as he spoke. "Here travelers see the Master in many ways and sing many songs. Do not expect to sing the same song you sang yesterday or the song you will sing tomorrow. Remember the little bird—she knows what to sing and where to sing it. You had best be on your way now, the Master is waiting for you."

CHAPTER 18

The Gardens of Devotion

—◦•◦—

The warm sun glowed brilliantly against the deep blue sky as the number of travelers in the gardens multiplied with each passing hour. Long lines stood outside a few of the gardens, especially the Garden of Joyful Surrender and the Garden of Great Thanksgiving. Wide colorful banners hung over their gateways and greeter hearts gave each traveler a friendly handshake as he or she stepped through the entrances.

Stone, brick, and wood-paneled walls enclosed a great many of the open-air gardens. Inside, seating areas surrounded central platforms. A handful of gardens were like the Garden of Contemplation—small, obscure, and hidden away behind natural shrubs and trees. Regardless of its composition, size, or location, every garden resonated with devotional activities. Outside the gardens, in the narrow side streets, all the sounds blended together in a great chorus of devotion for the Master.

Once inside any particular garden, the boundaries provided a haven from the multiplicity of worship styles and the traveler could concentrate on each garden's singular expression. Indeed, the Master's Gardens of Devotion were like a vast flower garden. The variety far exceeded anything that the three of them had ever experienced. Great choirs sang, musicians played their instruments, dancers danced, and actors portrayed dramatic scenes from the Great Book. People declared their love for the Master both together and privately. Many seemed to need the help of leaders, choirs, and musicians, while others made their devotions quite independently.

"These gardens are very much like the meeting places back home, don't you think, Hungry Heart?" Hopeful Heart inquired, peering inside the

Garden of Choral Exultation to see a large choir practicing for a presentation and musicians tuning up their instruments.

The sign on the door indicated that this garden had been reserved for evening devotions only. A broad-shouldered contentious heart stopped them from entering.

"Come back later. We are practicing now, and unless you are willing to submit yourself to a lengthy course of musical training to take part in our presentation, you had best leave now. We have a great deal of work to do. We try very hard to give only excellence to the Master. He deserves nothing less, you know."

Stepping back, the three companions raised their eyebrows, shrugged their shoulders, and continued to wander about. As they walked, Hungry Heart answered Hopeful Heart's question.

"In some ways, yes, these gardens are like the meeting places, but I don't see any elders here. Everyone is dressed in the same blue robes and everyone appears to be walking in the Master's authority. No one is teaching or expounding from the Great Book. Everyone is giving devotion to the Master—in one way or another," she added a bit sarcastically, as she glanced back in the contentious heart's direction.

"Do you believe how many people are here?" Trusting Heart gasped in wide-eyed wonder. "Everyone is singing to the Master."

"Everyone, that is, but us," Hungry Heart noted with a hint of desperation in her voice. The approaching sunset only increased her apprehension. "Hurry, it's getting late!" Hearing no response, she glanced back to find herself quite alone. Her two friends had literally disappeared from her sight!

How can they do this to me? How could they possibly leave me now? Hungry Heart called and called for her friends, as well as for the Master, but no one answered. The great chorus of praise rising to the sky above the gardens reduced her own voice to a whisper. Wisdom Heart's words echoed in her thoughts: "The little bird knows where to sing and what song to sing…he knows where his nest is."

Birds! What do I know about birds? They just fly here and there. They don't have to worry about anything but finding bugs and worms to eat. How am I supposed to find the Master while thinking about birds?

Hungry Heart kicked her foot against a rocky garden wall and then sat down beside it to indulge in a little self-pity. Now what am I supposed to do? she fussed, kicking off her sandals and nestling her bare feet in the soft green grass. "Maybe I should just pick a garden and do what everyone else is doing? I'll shout with the rockers or jump with the jumpers. Maybe I'll even stand on my head..." she mused aloud.

"Do? Devotion isn't something you 'do,' and standing on your head is only going to make you dizzy. Devotion is something you 'give.' Now what do you have to give to the Master, Hungry Heart?"

Hungry Heart gasped in surprise and looked up to see the old woman standing over her—the same one who had sent them to Wisdom Heart. Hungry Heart took a closer look at the woman. Ah, this was a counselor heart, someone who helped others to understand their own heart.

"Oh, Counselor Heart, I am so glad to see you!"

"What do you have to give, Hungry Heart?" the counselor heart interrupted. "Until you see this, you will sit here against this wall, and the flowers will grow up between your toes."

Hungry Heart lowered her eyes and looked away. "I have nothing left to give him. The little that I did have went to the Master's fire in the Great Refinery. The clothes I wear belong to him. The Great Book I carry belongs to him. These few crumbs of bread in my pocket belong to him. What do I possibly have to give? Why, even my paradigm pieces belong to him."

Counselor Heart smiled. "I think you have more than you know, although it is up to you to find it. You don't need me or anyone else right now and don't worry about your friends. They didn't leave you. They simply heard the song they needed to sing and followed it, just as you must do. I'm sure you will meet up with them again from time to time. I'll be going now and, by the way, watch those toes of yours. The flowers do grow quickly around here."

Hungry Heart pulled her bare feet back under her blue coat and sat quietly as the evening sky grew dark. The tall torches on the garden walls provided enough light for her to watch the stream of travelers continue to move in and out of the gardens throughout the night. Their faces radiated with love for the Master and their eyes—yes, there was something about their eyes. It was if they could see wonders too marvelous for words to express. She fell asleep leaning against the garden wall trying to figure out what everyone except she could see.

Very early the next morning, at dawn's first light, the blue bird's song awoke her. *Strange,* thought Hungry Heart, still a bit groggy, everyone must be asleep. *The only sound I hear is coming from that little bird.* Lifting its wings, the bird flew away, but Hungry Heart kept hearing the song. She started to hum a few notes as she sat there by the wall. By and by the little song gave her the courage to slip her sandals back on, get up, and try to find her way. The catchy little tune tugged at her harder and harder as she walked, until a waterfall of emotions spilled out from someplace within her heart. Hesitantly at first, and then with increasing confidence, she tried to express her feelings.

Words streaming from my heart, tears welling up within
Oh where, oh where do I begin, to tell you of my love for you?
Feelings rising up inside of me, turning round and round,
Waiting, waiting for a sound, to tell you of my love for you.
I lift up my hands as incense, my voice as a morning sacrifice...

She knew, from someplace deep inside her heart, that this song would lead her to a garden where she could lay her devotion at the Master's feet. Traveling in and around the maze of garden walls, her buoyant heart carried her step by step. Eventually she reached a small garden bordered only by folds of sheer white fabric draped from blossoming fig trees. A simple gold plate at the entrance read, "The Garden of Awesome Wonder."

Inside, men and women knelt in devotion. Others stood with uplifted arms, and quite a few sat on wooden benches. Over to one side, three men lay motionless on the ground. The only sound Hungry Heart heard was the song in her own heart. She found an empty place on a nearby bench and sat quietly with her eyes closed, but within moments she fell to her knees and lifted her own arms up in adoration. The fact that she did not see the Master did not disturb her. She felt his presence, and she knew that he could see and hear her. That was the reality her heart reached out for—her Master, alive, watching her and receiving her gift of devotion.

Her hand reached for the paradigm pouch hanging over her heart. Pulling it up over her head, she held it up to the blue sky, weeping, "Master, all that I have learned, all the truth that you have given me, does not compare to this moment with you. You are so much more than I have ever dared to imagine. You deserve every song that comes forth from these gardens— and so much more. You are too awesome and too wonderful for words!"

"Hungry Heart," the Master's voice spoke kindly from the sky above, "you have given me a beautiful gift of devotion, and I am pleased to have it here in my gardens. The song rooted in your heart is ready to be planted here. It will grow and grow and grow, in an eternal bloom, a fragrant blossom, to represent your love for me. Each time I walk through my gardens, it will be here and I will remember your devotion."

Hungry Heart pinched her eyes closed just as tightly as she could, afraid to lose this awesome moment and never be able to capture it again. If her life ended here, now, it would be enough to be in the Master's presence and to sense his sincere delight in her small gift.

Like an ocean wave returning again and again to the shore, Hungry Heart's emotions and thoughts moved in rhythm to the Master's love. She heard his voice speak again.

"Now, I am going to ask you to open your eyes, and as you do, I do not want you to look back. I want you to look at me, just as I am before you now."

Her eyes opened to see the Master standing before her, clothed in beautiful garments. A crown of gold sat above his forehead, and a magnificent red, blue, and purple robe flowed down to his feet. Over his robe, a gem-studded gold breastplate covered his upper body, and in his right hand he held a golden incense burner. His countenance glowed with a translucent shimmer, yet he stood before her with the same eyes of compassion and love that she had known all her life. Speechless and somewhat afraid to see the Master in such majesty, Hungry Heart fell to the ground at his feet and did not move.

"Hungry Heart, do not be afraid. Your devotion and your song of love has lifted me from the one who walked by your side over the mountains to the one you see before you now. I have always been your King as well as your Master, and I will always be. Here, in the Garden of Awesome Wonder, you behold me as you do because your heart has opened to receive a deeper revelation of my Lordship in the kingdom of Christianity."

"Oh, Master...I mean, your Majesty!" His presence left her speechless. Nothing, absolutely nothing, could be said to describe the glory prevailing in this garden and her heart. Her stammers turned to tears, then to her song of adoration, and then back to tears again.

He touched her shoulder and asked her to rise. As she did, he placed a miniature incense burner in her hand. "Always remember, the incense burning in the Gardens of Devotion comes from your heart. The fire that burns this incense comes from my Great Refinery. I wait for your devotion just as you wait for me. Your heart will see me in proportion to the incense burning in your heart."

With those words, he left—or the vision of him did. Hungry Heart was not certain exactly what had happened, but the paradigm piece lay in her hand. Trembling, she leaned back against a pink flowering dogwood tree.

Hungry Heart had known the Master since childhood; he had always been there for her family. His lordship over the kingdom of Christianity and her life stood without question. She had seen and heard him in many ways since her rite of dedication at the meeting place. Never had she questioned the validity of her relationship with him.

The Master was as real to her as her parents or Grandfather Humble Heart were. True, he moved in a greater and far more powerful dimension than she did, but he had great responsibilities over the land and needed to be able to come and go in the blink of an eye. There were many people to care for, guide, and encourage from the Mountains of Joy to the Valley of Despair, so he needed to be able to be seen by everyone at different times and in different ways. It was a paradox—the Master was like everyone else, yet at the same time he far exceeded the realm of human possibility.

Until she had reached the City of Bread, she thought she knew exactly who he was and who she was. Her relationship with him had always existed solely in what she had learned about him and the times she could see him with her or hear him speaking to her. The City of Bread had stretched her understanding to accept knowing him in the lives of others as well.

Now, here in the Gardens of Devotion, something changed. She had known for years that he was King as well as Master of all Christianity. This fact was not new to her. Long ago, as a very young child, she had witnessed a grand processional with her parents. The Master had been dressed in royal robes that flowed through the streets. Yet, even that experience paled in comparison to this. Today she not only had seen his sovereignty, but also experienced it. His presence had totally engulfed her with his grandeur and exceeding greatness.

"Devotion opens our hearts in new ways, doesn't it," said Trusting Heart sweetly from the other side of the tree where she had been singing her own song for the Master. "My love for the Master is deeper now than I ever dreamed possible. He is the faithful one. I am only a dim reflection in comparison to him. I have seen my heart in the light of his glory, and I can do nothing less than to bow down and worship him."

"Trusting Heart! Oh, I am so glad that I found you! Look, we both ended up here in the same garden and at the very same tree. I cannot describe what I have seen, but surely you already know the Master's glorious splendor…" Hungry Heart rambled on in hushed tones, too excited to keep quiet. The two friends stepped outside the gate to avoid disturbing anyone else's devotions.

"I wonder," Trusting Heart considered, "if there are other songs in our hearts and other gardens to visit, or if we are supposed to stay here in this one? What do you think, Hungry Heart?"

Just the possibility of increasing her devotion to the Master sounded like an invitation Hungry Heart could not refuse.

"Well, we will never find out standing here. Go, my friend. Follow the songs in your heart and explore as many gardens as you possibly can. I will do the same. Perhaps we will meet again. But more importantly, the Master is waiting for us."

The two friends listened to their hearts quietly together and then slowly stepped apart, each to the music of her own song. Trusting Heart stepped into the Garden of Faithful Remembrance not far away while Hungry Heart followed a small footpath down the hill and off to the right in response to the melody burning inside her.

The refiner's fire is burning; inside my heart is turning;
I am longing, longing, longing for your fire to burn in me.
Your flames of love well tended, I am ready to surrender...

Hungry Heart stopped at the Garden of Refining Fire and listened to the words rising up from her own heart. Bewildered by her own devotions and unable to see beyond the high stone walls, she hesitated at the garden gate for a second before she reprimanded herself. Nonsense. I am not afraid of the Master's fire. If it belongs to him, it is a good place to be. Tentatively, she stepped inside the gate, expecting to see others there also.

To her surprise, she found herself quite alone and inside a most unusual garden. It was, in fact, more like a wide, circular, walled-in courtyard than a garden. Instead of trees, shrubs and flowers, smooth flat red stones created wide circles around the very center, where a small flame burned inside a golden vessel. Hungry Heart stepped toward the center with her eyes fixed on the fire and continued to sing the melody in her heart. At first the garden's center and the fire burning there seemed to be very small and only a few steps away, but it did not take her long to realize that the fire burned a great distance away.

The refiner's fire is burning; inside my heart is turning;
I am longing, longing, longing for your fire to burn in me.
Your flames of love well tended, I am ready to surrender...

The longer Hungry Heart walked, the more intense her desire to reach the fire became. She tried to run, but the slow rhythm in her heart slowed her down again and again, enticing her to step slowly and deliberately over the red stones beneath her feet. Rational thought told her to turn around and leave the garden immediately, to go back to the lush green Gardens of Praise and Thanksgiving or to the wonderful Garden of Awesome Wonder. However, the song burning in her heart gave her no choice. She had to reach the fire, regardless of the cost.

Although the fire did not look any larger or appear any closer, the red stones beneath her feet started to feel warmer. Over and over she sang the little melody. As she sang, she understood only one thing—she needed to reach the fire to lay her devotion at the Master's feet. The narrowing circles gave her only one route to the fire, however. There were no shortcuts. She had to continue to walk straight in. If she detoured to the right or to the left, she would end up going in circles.

Hours passed, yet no one else entered the garden. Nor did she see the Master. Only the illusive, small red flame burned in the never-ending distance. Once, looking back, Hungry Heart realized that she had gone too far to see the gate. On and on she went, her desperation to reach the flame mingling with the heat rising from the red stones. Together they seemed to turn the garden into a hazy maze of red ripples in an ever-widening sea that she had to cross in order to give the ultimate gift of devotion.

Hungry Heart sang about the fire, for the fire, to the fire, and sometimes, it seemed, with the fire. It did not make any sense, but she had left sense at the gate long ago. Understanding did not belong in this garden anymore than flowers did. No, this garden had been designed to consume her hungry heart, not feed it. With each step her longing turned to groaning and her groaning to deep painful moaning.

Finally, taking one last exhausted and desperate step, she fell forward and cried out, "Master, I have failed. Forgive me! I cannot reach the fire to give you my devotion!"

Dazed and too weak to go on, she watched the fire grow larger and larger. Circle by circle it grew until she realized that it was burning outward to meet her! Within seconds it had swept over her body and engulfed her in its flames—then disappeared as quickly as it had appeared. That was the last she remembered for a long while.

"Hungry Heart, are you all right?" a mercy heart massaged her temples and smoothed the hair back from her face. "Everyone has been so worried about you. It's been days since you stumbled out of the Garden of Refining Fire. Please, say something, or we shall have to take you back to the Valley to recover."

Hungry Heart looked up to see a circle of friends gathered around her. They were all there—Hopeful Heart, Trusting Heart, Faithful Heart, Devoted Heart, Wisdom Heart, Counselor Heart, and even Contentious Heart. She smiled weakly and begged, "No, no, please do not take me back to the Valley. I have to...I have to continue my journey to the Third Mountain. I heard the Master speak to me in the refining fire...I don't remember what he said. But I must complete my paradigm quest."

With that, she fell asleep again. The mercy heart assured everyone with a smile, "She will be fine. She will never be the same again—no one who comes out of that garden ever is, but she will be just fine. The Master spoke to her, and his words will keep her heart steady, regardless of what lies ahead."

PART FOUR

THE

Third Mountain

CHAPTER 19

Impossible Possibilities

————◆◆◆————

The mercy heart's words proved to be true. Hungry Heart rarely spoke about her experience in the garden because she simply did not know what happened, how it happened, or why it happened. She could not even remember what the Master had said as the fire rushed over her, only that he had met her at her point of surrender.

The longer she stayed in the Gardens of Devotion, the more people she met with similar experiences. They, too, said little about the encounter, except, "I've been through the fire." Others nodded knowingly. Nothing more needed to be said.

One morning Hungry Heart sat cross-legged on the ground in her favorite spot, a quiet refuge in the Garden of Surrender under the almond trees. There, she remembered the forgotten words from the midst of the fire.

"Hungry Heart, I have prepared your heart to receive that which you do not understand. Come with me to the Third Mountain, beyond the veil of your understanding, and into my throne room."

Without hesitation, Hungry Heart rose to her feet and started walking east toward the edge of the Gardens of Devotion. This time she did not need to wait for traveling companions or even to catch a glimpse of the Master leading the way. The figure of a man failed to contain her growing awareness of his majesty. In some mysterious way, he lived both within her and around her. His presence stretched from one end of the world to the next, from the highest heavens to the deepest seas.

Hungry Heart moved past familiar gardens and waved to friends.

Encouraging hearts waved her on, and a few curious hearts followed her for a while until they grew tired and turned back. Ahead of her, however, a group of critical hearts waited. It was almost as if they had expected her to pass their way. Without even inquiring about her journey, one after another snapped at her like hungry fish leaping out of the water for bait.

"Where do you think you're going? How can you possibly believe you are prepared for such a journey? You had better turn back right now or you will find yourself in the border countries! Go back, Hungry Heart, to where you belong. Stop trying to be something that you are not. Give it up. Travelers are not meant to journey alone like this. You don't have any friends with you, and we certainly don't see the Master by your side."

In times past, such critical objections might have dissuaded her. Today she merely smiled and remembered the well-meaning cautious hearts who had warned her about venturing as far as the Second Mountain. Without stopping to argue, she waved and left them standing in the middle of the road, looking quite dumbfounded.

The roadway before Hungry Heart soon narrowed to an obscure trail through the woods. Time after time, the path itself disappeared, forcing her to depend upon the eyes of her heart to lead her through the dense under-brush.

Eventually, late in the afternoon, she pushed aside a low-hanging tree limb and stepped out onto a narrow precipice. A gorge separated the two mountains, and the only way across was a long footbridge swinging in the wind. Across the bridge, Hungry Heart could see the gateway to the Third Mountain waiting for her. *Oh my,* she rejoiced, *this has been much easier than I dared imagine. I can be on the Third Mountain before nightfall!*

Evidently the bridge had not been used very much. Wild vines embraced the loose wooden planks and twined around badly weathered side ropes. All in all, the footbridge did not appear to be very safe. "No," her voice echoed in the canyon beneath her. "I have come this far, and I will not go back. The Master has called me to the Third Mountain, and I am going to go!" After one deep confident breath, she stepped onto the swinging bridge.

Carefully she picked her way from plank to plank. When she reached midway over the deep canyon, a gust of wind whipped underneath the bridge. Swinging wildly under its force, the tossing bridge threw her against the braided side ropes. Clutching the threadbare ropes as tightly as possible and slowly sinking to her knees, Hungry Heart's confidence gave way to fear as she envisioned herself falling into the silent depths beneath her.

"Master!" she weakly cried, as if her own voice might break the last thin ropes holding the bridge together. "Master, I need you...please do not leave me here now." Only the wind answered her as it whipped the long narrow bridge again, rolling it from side to side.

Hungry Heart crawled forward, inches at a time, until a gaping hole directly in her path stopped her. It looked huge. How could she cross such an impassable distance? The situation seemed impossible. The wind slowly died down as Hungry Heart concentrated on the Master's call to the Third Mountain. Eventually the bridge hung still. Then, refusing to look at the impossible circumstances any longer, Hungry Heart stood to her feet and stretched out one leg as far as possible over the foreboding empty space.

Thump! Her right foot touched solid wood! Then so did the left! Miraculously, she made her way to secure ground on the Third Mountain. She almost couldn't believe it. Just as she turned to look back at the bridge, a loud crack of thunder shook the mountain. The last ropes snapped under its force, plunging the bridge into the canyon. Suddenly weak-kneed, Hungry Heart slumped to the ground.

"Hungry Heart, remember my words...I will take you so far that you will never be able to go back."

The memory of Prophetic Heart's words rushed in and stabbed her heart like a sharp sword. Any chance of returning to her family, her homeland or any of the wonderful people on the First and Second Mountain disappeared with the bridge's collapse. For some reason, far beyond her understanding, it seemed as though her last connection to the past had just been ripped away. Before she had time to mentally process her circumstances, a tall, distinguished white-robed woman extended her hand.

"Hungry Heart, welcome to the Third Mountain. I know you find yourself in a most difficult place right now, but don't worry about the bridge. Don't even think about it. It served its purpose—it carried you here. This is where you have been longing to come, isn't it?"

Nodding silently, Hungry Heart glanced once more at the remnants of the bridge still dangling on the other side, then turned her attention to the gate before her. Long tightly interwoven vines with colorful blue, purple, red, and white flowers cascaded down the mountainside and created a majestic curtain, a natural forest tapestry that parted just slightly in the center and exposed minute rays of brilliant light. Without thinking, she reached forward to expose the source of the light, but the assistant's hand stopped her just in time with a word of caution.

"No, not yet, Hungry Heart. First you must prepare yourself to enter this gate. Only those with clean hands and a pure heart may approach the Master's Third Mountain. Come, sit down over here, and let me explain."

As Hungry Heart sat down on a wide seat carved into the mountainside, the assistant continued.

"During the old times in the Fatherland, only the highest assistants were permitted beyond this gate—and then only one day a year. On that day, the designated assistant prepared himself with ritual washings and devotions. It was a high and honored privilege to be chosen as the representative to bow before the Master. In those days, the Master rarely walked among the people as he does now. No, in those days he spent most of his time here upon his golden throne, speaking only to those devoted enough to enter his presence. Most of those who entered returned with a message for the people who waited outside. There were times, however, when the one who entered was never seen nor heard from again. The Great Book tells that it was a most fearful experience and that only the strongest hearts survived the Master's awesome presence.

"After the Great Revolt when the Master returned alive, his golden throne became a throne of fire. He decreed the way to be opened for all citizens to enter, at any time, to speak with him about any concern without fear. He never wants to be separated from his citizens again, and he has provided the way for you to enter this great and awesome dwelling. It is, however, up to you to prepare your heart."

"I have traveled a great distance to be here, and I will do whatever the Master requires of me," replied Hungry Heart confidently.

"First you must remove your blue coat of authority. Only clean white garments such as the ones you received on the First Mountain are allowed here."

"You want me to remove my blue coat? But the Master himself gave it to me. How will anyone recognize that I belong to him and that I have the authority to speak in his behalf if I have no blue coat?"

"The only authority that exists on the Third Mountain comes directly from the Master. This mountain is his throne room, the innermost sanctuary of his dwelling place. It will not be necessary for anyone to recognize you, your place of service, or even your journey. The Master will know that you are present, and that will be quite enough for him. Will that be enough for you, Hungry Heart? Are you willing to lay aside your own ambitions as well as your blue coat of authority?"

Hungry Heart bit her lip tightly. She did not want to refuse, but the blue coat had become so much a part of her identity. How could she possibly part with it now? In the midst of her dilemma she spotted a few other travelers listening to the same instructions from another assistant. "How did they get here if the bridge is gone?" she puzzled aloud. "No one came over it with me."

The assistant laughed knowingly. "Oh, travelers come here in many ways. Some have climbed from the canyon below, others have followed the river road, and a few have come here in giant balloon baskets. There's just no end to the ways the Master beckons for hearts to meet him here."

"Balloon baskets...river roads...! Why, I nearly fell to my death on that threadbare bridge! Why did I have to..."

The assistant held up her hand and stopped her question. "The Master called you across the bridge. Your heart responded. That is the beginning and the end of the matter, isn't it?"

Accepting the gentle rebuke with one eye and watching a fellow traveler hand over his blue coat with the other, Hungry Heart slipped her own blue coat over her head. She touched the fabric tenderly, remembering the intense joy she had felt when she received it at the gateway to the Second Mountain. It all seemed so far away now, yet the coat still looked new. She handed it over with tear-filled eyes. She did not understand, but she remembered the Master's words "...to accept that which you do not understand...."

"There's one more thing," the assistant said somewhat hesitantly. "You must also leave your paradigm pieces here with me."

Hungry Heart's eyes flashed in outright defiance. "No! There must be some mistake. No one ever relinquishes his or her paradigm pieces of truth. The rite of dedication warned me, 'Never let these pieces depart from you. Keep them close to your heart.' How can you possibly expect me to leave them here? My entire journey has one purpose—to complete my paradigm quest!"

The assistant stepped in front of the vine-covered gate as if to block it from Hungry Heart's path. "The choice, as always, is yours, Hungry Heart. You may stay right here with your paradigm pieces, or you may give them to me and approach the Third Mountain. I know you do not understand, but you will in time. Your paradigm collection is very precious, but it is something that will only hinder your journey here. The Master's truth lies in pieces written in your heart, but pieces of his truth will take you only so far. They will not take you past this gateway. Just as your rite of dedication did not prepare you for many of the adventures you have had on your journey, so your pieces will not help you here."

Hungry Heart reached up to touch the blue bag over her heart. She fingered the delicate paradigm pieces through the fabric. The sheer impossibility of handing them over stunned her into silence. *This collection represents my entire life with the Master, she wondered silently. How can this possibly be the Master's desire? I must be certain...*

"Please, may I have some time to consider this? I know that I do not understand many things, but I must hear the Master give his approval. This is very important, and as much as I respect your position here at the gateway, I do not want to make a mistake."

Relaxing her somewhat formal posture, the assistant agreed. "Of course, take all the time you need. I will be here when you are ready, but remember, the bridge is gone."

Hungry Heart shut her eyes and concentrated very hard with the unspoken question in her heart. Although she did not see him, she heard the Master's clear voice interrupt her own thoughts.

"Hungry Heart, the paradigm pieces are very precious. I am pleased that you have treasured them close to your heart and shared them with so many. Now I want to give you greater portions of truth—more than will fill a dozen paradigm pouches; more than your hands can carry. One day you will understand, but for now, I must ask you to accept that which you do not understand. Leave them here and follow me to the Third Mountain."

"But, Master, what about my completed paradigm...my appointment in your service...my paradigm quest...?"

"All this and more, you must be willing to leave outside this gate. Nothing, absolutely nothing, comes through the third gateway but your devotion and love for me. You must learn that I am all and in all. I am everything you need. I want to be your quest."

With those words, Hungry Heart opened her eyes and untied the golden cord from around her neck. She carefully handed the assistant the small blue pouch bulging with the precious pieces that represented all that she had and all that she had ever hoped to be.

Just then her old friend, Sacrificial Heart, stepped from under the trees. She put her finger to Hungry Heart's lips before she could say anything. "Hush now, Hungry Heart. This is not the time for questions. We are under a vow of silence from this moment on. It does not matter how I came here. What matters is that I am here now, and that I am here to help you wash, just as we did in the Lagoon of Truth. Come with me to the River of His Mercy. Remember, do not speak. Your heart must be silent in order for the Waters of Unending Mercy to reach the deepest places in your life. The Master knows what needs to be known, and he will give you truth as you are willing to receive it."

Taking Hungry Heart by the hand, Sacrificial Heart led her down a tree-lined path to a secluded riverbank, where they bathed in the Master's River of Mercy. Stepping from the water, they changed into sparkling clean white garments. Still under a vow of silence, they returned to the gateway where Sacrificial Heart placed Hungry Heart's hand in the assistant's and then stepped back quietly.

Hungry Heart contemplated whether or not she should wait until morning before passing through the third gate. The sun was already slipping behind the western mountain ridges. Nevertheless, the assistant motioned her through the gateway. No longer under the vow of silence, the assistant told her, "Do not be concerned about the darkness, Hungry Heart. The night may be very long, but morning will come. When it does, you will be thankful for the darkness."

CHAPTER 20

The Long Dark Night

From her first steps through the third gateway, the Third Mountain proved to be everything and more Hungry Heart had ever hoped or longed for. Everyone and everything moved in perfect harmony and contentment under the Master's authority. The glow from his throne room covered the mountain with soft iridescent rainbows of light both day and night. Flowers turned their faces to greet his light and fruit trees continually yielded their bounty year round. Animals roamed freely, at peace with each other and with man. Waterfalls spilled from the mountaintops into crystal clear rivers, streams, and pools. Gentle, soothing sounds from nature continually filled the air like a finely tuned, well-orchestrated symphony of life.

Fresh fruits and delicious foods were always at hand, and no one ever grew weary, irritable or contentious. The fact that every heart belonged solely to the Master eliminated all manners of strife and competition. Travelers moved from place to place on the mountain with ease and never suffered physical afflictions.

The Master provided for every need. Small intimate groups formed from time to time to join their voices in devotion to the Master, their hearts blending with praise and thanksgiving for his unending mercy and goodness. Men, women and children lifted their hands toward his throne room high up in the mountains. Sometimes they sat quietly for hours, simply listening to the sound of his voice or the music he created in the wind.

More than once Hungry Heart wondered if she had left the earth and stepped into the Master's heavens. His voice would respond before she finished thinking of her questions, and he filled her heart with deep under-

147

standing and wisdom as he spoke. One word from him stilled hundreds of questions in her heart.

Day after day, she investigated this wonderful place and shared delightful moments with other travelers. Even though she had been reluctant to leave her blue coat and paradigm pieces at the gateway, she found that no one cared about names, positions or even the paradigm pieces that once had occupied so much of their time together. The only name that mattered was the Master's, and everyone lived securely in his undivided love for all. Hearts helped and encouraged one another without question. If anyone lacked, in any way at all, the Master used someone close by to be his hands and feet to meet the need.

The "needs" here on the Third Mountain proved to be very different from those back on the Plains of Hope—or even on the First and Second Mountains. Back there, needs represented emptiness in one's life, whether material, physical, or emotional. They were met by feeding and clothing the needy, encouraging the weak, and giving mercy to the sick. Here on the Third Mountain, the Master provided all these things and more. The only need or lack that any heart experienced was the need to give more of his or her heart in devotion to the Master. Thus Hungry Heart often helped others to listen to him, just by sitting with them quietly and enjoying the wonders of his presence. Others, in turn, helped her to lift her voice in adoration or to playfully rejoice with the children.

Hungry Heart believed that her paradigm quest had ended, if she happened to think about it at all. How could anything be more perfect than this, and how could she possibly belong anywhere else but here on the Third Mountain? There were times, of course, that she missed her family and friends. At such times she would ask the Master to call them to the Third Mountain, too. She wanted to share this heavenly life with all of them just as soon as possible. Still, these thoughts were few and short-lived because the Master always held preeminence in her heart. For the most part, her devotion and love for him reached out to embrace other travelers in marvelous ways. Never had she felt so complete, so fulfilled, or so at peace with herself and others.

One of Hungry Heart's favorite places was a wide, beautiful blue mountain lake at the base of the highest peak. Boat excursions often carried travelers out on the lake to give them a dazzling glimpse of the Master's mountaintop throne room. If Hungry Heart stood on the bow of the boat, heading east, she could see his throne cast a beam of light beyond description. Not even the sun compared to the radiance streaming from his mountaintop.

Normally the boats headed in an easterly direction until the intense light forced them to pull about and head west again. No one, at least no one Hungry Heart knew about, had ever climbed to the very top of the mountain. Some said that his throne actually sat in the heavens beyond the doors of death. Others whispered, "There is a way, one that no one has ever returned to tell about." A few older hearts listened to the tales quietly, saying very little, if anything, about the possibility. Thankful for the opportunity to come as close to his throne as she could, Hungry Heart loved the boat trips and soaked up as much of his penetrating warm light as possible. Sometimes she actually had to close her eyes against the light's brightness just before the boat pulled about.

On one particular excursion, a strong wind blew in over the mountains and down across the lake. Within moments, the boat began to tumble back and forth in the shifting waves, which grew larger and larger until the high cascades of water battered the ship directly into the intense light. Everyone pleaded and cried out for the Master as the water beat unmercifully against the boat and long-forgotten fears resurfaced in their hearts. Desperately, people clung to anything within reach.

Back and forth the boat rocked until one traveler after another succumbed to seasickness. For the first time since their arrival on the Third Mountain, the travelers' bodies were racked with nausea, dizziness, and pain. Hungry Heart struggled to hold on to a side rail as fatigue began creeping through her limbs. *What's happening?* Her heart nearly burst with fear at every heartbeat. *Where are you, Master? Do you want us to perish?*

Another passenger called out, "I speak to the wind and the waves and I command you to stop in the Master's name. We are his people, and we dwell here on the Third Mountain!" The wind only blew harder until its roar drowned out the voice. Hungry Heart groaned in despair. *If only we had our blue coats, we could speak in the Master's name! If he does not rescue us soon, we will all perish.*

The angry, white-capped waves crashed like mountain waterfalls. She trembled and hung on as tight as she could. Just then a horrific crack of lightning ripped through the skies and struck the center mast. Stunned, Hungry Heart lost her grip on the handrail and fell backwards into the water. Flailing wildly, she sank beneath the surface. With one last desperate attempt to survive, she kicked her way upwards through the waves and grabbed a small piece of the boat's splintered hull. Gasping for precious breath, she pulled herself halfway out of the water onto the wood, dazed and disoriented.

As the storm died down in intensity, Hungry Heart continued to cling to her small, makeshift raft. When it was gone, intense heat began to beat down on the water, and the current pulled her directly into the brilliant light. Warm blood oozed from a gash over her right eye, and her head throbbed painfully at each lap of the water. No one else was in sight. Weak, trembling with fear, and in tears, Hungry Heart tried to turn her back to the stream of light. When that failed, she shut her eyes as tightly as she could and wrapped one arm over her head to protect herself against the intense light. From a distance the Master's light had been soft, beautiful, and comforting. Now it blinded her.

I must have floated too far away from the Third Mountain, her disoriented thoughts rambled, or this must be a dream, a very bad dream, and I will wake up again....I know I will. Her hand instinctively reached for her paradigm pieces before she remembered they weren't there. Panic seized her. Here she was—alone, hurt, and probably near death—without her paradigm pieces.

How did this happen? "Oh Master, where are you?" she pleaded. "I cannot see...I cannot hear your voice in my heart, and I do not understand what's happening to me. Please, have mercy upon me and rescue me!"

Just then her splinter of a raft bumped up against something hard, then scraped against a rock. "Land! I am on land! Oh, thank you, Master...thank you. Forgive me for doubting you."

Exhausted, but thankful to be back on land, Hungry Heart inched her way off the raft and cautiously crawled over sharp rocks on her hands and knees. She could see only a few inches at a time as she squinted and tried to protect her eyes from the blinding light. Once she got past the barrier reef rocks, she reached a beach of smooth sea-washed stones instead of sand. Stumbling with pain and fatigue, Hungry Heart gave in to her body's demands and fell under waves of semi-consciousness on the hard pebble beach.

Hours passed. When Hungry Heart regained consciousness, she automatically opened her eyes, but the light forced her to close them again. Perhaps the Master will send a mercy heart to help me, she thought hopefully. No one came to her rescue as she lay there, but the light, which denied her sight, had dried her clothing and hair as well as heated the pebbles to just the right temperature to warm and soothe her aching body.

Feeling stronger with every passing moment, but still unable to see clearly, Hungry Heart slowly got up and made her way inland. She spied some thick, wide-leafed bushes ahead, and an idea struck her. Perhaps she could use the leaves to cover her eyes! Quickly she gathered a few broad leaves and fashioned a mask. Tying them around her head with a piece of linen from her torn sleeve, she peeked out carefully. Yes, it worked perfectly! The thick leaves protected her eyes from the dazzling light while allowing her to peek underneath to see one step at a time.

This does not make any sense at all, she tried to reason. *The Master has promised never to leave me or forsake me, yet here I am, so close to his light that I cannot even see where I am going, and there's no one here to help me. What good is the light if it does not show me the way? I am like a blind man groping in the night shadows. At least back on the Plains of Hope I had neighbors and friends...even Loving Heart came to help me. Here I am completely alone, abandoned in this dark night. Yet he promised...*

Hungry Heart refused to finish her thoughts. No, she refused to think anything but hopeful thoughts about the Master. He would come, she just knew he would. He had to!

The brilliant light continued to penetrate the deep tropical foliage she trudged through, but the cool green leaves did make it easier to manage. After only a few hours, she reached a small clearing canopied by large low-hanging willow trees. A clear stream ran nearby. Falling face down into the stream for a drink of water, Hungry Heart took a long drink of the refreshing water. After satisfying her thirst, she slumped back underneath a tree and wept. "Oh, Master, what have I done to displease you? Please tell me. Show me where I have failed you."

She tried to recite paradigm truth from memory, but the words all jumbled together. In an attempt to figure out where she had gone wrong, she retraced each step of her journey, one by one, mentally recounting conversations with the Master and with fellow travelers. Like a detective searching for any minuscule clue, she examined and reexamined every word, every encounter, every lesson learned—anything to help her understand.

She tried to sing, but she could not hear the song in her heart over her yearnings to be back on the Plains of Hope, the First Mountain, or even the Second Mountain—anywhere but in the dark shadows where she sat. *Oh, to see the Master again,* her heart ached. *To feel the touch of his hand on my shoulders, to see the look in his eyes, to hear the sound of his voice.*

Thud! Thud! Thud! Suddenly a gust of wind beat a loose branch against the sticks beside it. The peculiar thumping noise brought Hungry Heart to her feet. It sounded hollow. Hungry Heart cautiously followed the sound. Groping with her hands in front of her, her fingers encountered a small lean-to, built from tree limbs and covered with dried leafy branches. Someone else is here! Her heart leaped with joyful expectation.

Sliding inside the primitive dwelling, her hopes both rose and plummeted. The covering provided just enough protection from the light for her to uncover her eyes and see for a small distance. That was a relief! However, she quickly realized that no one had been inside the little thatched tent for a long, long time. Feeling desperate, she explored every dark corner for something—anything—frantically rooting out tiny growing plants as if trying to reclaim this small patch for humanity. As she did, she found a large leather pouch buried underneath a mat of twisted vines!

Unable to contain her excitement, Hungry Heart squealed in delight and opened the worn leather bag with trembling hands. Someone, long ago, had left a few torn pages from the Great Book and a hand-written journal. Just touching this link with another traveler gave her reason to smile. At first it seemed quite impossible to read the brittle pages, but eventually her eyes adapted and she treasured every word, devouring them like a true hungry heart.

Day 1: The waves have carried me here to this cruel fate. I believe a band of spirit creatures from the border countries plotted against me. I lost all my paradigm pieces at sea, but surely the Master will rescue me at any moment. I have worked in his fields for many years, and I know that he will reward my faithfulness. He will not disappoint me.

Day 6: Will this darkness ever end? Will the light ever give way for my sight again? I continue to call for the Master, but the seas are silent. My body is in pain and the small amount of food that I am able to find here is barely sufficient to keep me alive. I fear that I will perish here. The light that I reached for has become my darkness.

Time unknown: I have been in this darkness for a very long time now, and I believe I am beginning to understand the Master's wisdom in bringing me here. The longer I remain, the less I long for those things he gave to me and the more I long for him. I have lost track of time. The feelings of abandonment were very strong in the beginning, but they have become less and less with each passing day.

At first I cried out to him with every breath, begging him to rescue me from this prison of darkness and to take me back to the harvest fields where I could prove my love and faithfulness to him. This morning my heart died to this desire, and all I am able to utter is one word, "Master, Master, Master." Oddly, this is enough.

Weeks have passed: I do not understand what is happening to me, but I know that I am changing. The darkness no longer threatens me. In some strange way, it has become my refuge from a life filled with dependence upon what I could see and feel. I know that he is here with me, but not in any of the ways that I have known thus far. If it were not for him, I should have perished long ago. He is here, sustaining me in the dark night.

Months later: I found a treasure today! Someone buried a few pages from the Great Book under a rock. What joy fills my heart as I read. It is different than I remember it from former days…or is it that I am different? I am reading that during the era of the Fatherland, the Master asked his people to dwell in tents such as this to celebrate his faithfulness each year. Celebrate? What does it truly mean? It used to be dancing and singing. Now it is simply knowing that he is and always will be enough.

A new day: I fell on my face before him today and begged him to forgive me for measuring the wideness of his mercy and love by my own understanding and my own desires. I am so small in comparison, as small as this tiny oasis in his great ocean of darkness. Yet, he loves me and continues to change my heart.

My final words: I do not know what morning will bring, but I do know that I am emerging from the darkened womb of my own understanding into new realities of his love. I leave these few thoughts here for anyone who travels behind me. Have courage, embrace the night and allow his love to embrace you until he calls you forth.

Hungry Heart read the journal entries over and over. The words gave her hope and a deep sense of peace. "I do not understand this darkness, but I will accept it as from his hand and stay here until the morning breaks," she promised herself aloud.

During the next few months, Hungry Heart held herself to that promise. She experienced bodily pain, hunger, loneliness, and troubling doubts. Her emotions urged her to rush headlong into the sea and dare the Master to save her from death, but her heart kept her still by repeating again and again, "Master, Master, Master." Just the sound of his name continued to be enough.

When she slept, her dreams took her back into the past and then plunged her forward into a strange future that did not fit the past. All her life she had been raised to believe that the pieces of her life would fit together and that she would receive her appointment in her service with her completed paradigm. Now, nothing fit together. Pieces of truth and her present experience challenged one another like light and darkness.

Bit by bit the raging tide of emotions subsided, and her heart settled into acceptance. A short time ago she might have described it as defeat. Defeat, however, would have carried her heart away from the Master's truth. Acceptance sent her into a dimension of his love that she had not even known existed—a place where nothing, absolutely nothing, could separate her from him. Here the Master's lordship in her life did not depend upon the present realities, her feelings, or even her understanding.

It does not matter, she admitted to herself, *whether I live or die; remain here in this darkness forever or leave; laugh again or dance; embrace my family or live with empty arms. The only thing that matters is that I am in my Master's hand, and he is in my heart.*

With those words echoing in her heart, a cheerful voice called to her from outside.

"Hungry Heart, come out! The boat is here, and it is time to continue your journey! Hurry now, you don't want to keep the Master waiting, do you?"

CHAPTER 21
The Appointment

"Are you going to stay in there for the rest of your life?" the voice called. "We have places to go and things to do! Come on, Hungry Heart!" A short, round-faced assistant poked his head inside the lean-to and offered his hand with a friendly grin.

Needless to say, his sudden appearance rather startled her. So much so, in fact, that she simply stared at his outstretched hand for a few moments before accepting it. Cautiously she stepped outside. For the first time in weeks—or was it months?—she could see without shielding her eyes!

Dozens of rainbows filled the bright blue sky, each one overlapping the next as if they were holding hands, creating ribbons of dancing colors. Beautiful, vivid scenes surrounded her in every direction. The trees, flowers, birds, and even the dirt she stood upon looked far more colorful than she had ever seen.

"The light?" Hungry Heart inquired. "The light was so bright that I could not see..."

"Perhaps you could not see because your eyes needed time to adjust to the Master's high mountain light, or perhaps you could not see because of the darkness in your own heart, or perhaps...oh, no matter! What matters now is that you *can* see and that you are ready to approach the Master's throne. He sent me to fetch you, and I assure you that it will be a most wonderful experience. Come now, we can't keep him waiting."

Hungry Heart followed the assistant out of the forest, past the pebble beach, and into a small boat on the calm blue-green lake waters. The Master's high throne room sparkled on the highest peak just across a small inlet. The thought of being so close to his throne and yet so far away spoke to her about her own life. There, in the darkened lean-to, her natural senses had felt so unattached to him, and yet, even during the darkest moments, her heart had clung to his love for her.

Hungry Heart could not help smiling as she followed the chubby little assistant. He waved his hands, laughed, and chatted endlessly about fetching travelers from this place and that place in his small rowboat. After they pushed off into the water, Hungry Heart held onto the sides with white knuckles. Even though her last boat ride felt like it was eons ago, the memory of the tempest and high waves was very vivid. However, it only took them a few minutes to reach the opposite shore where a long, flat-stoned stairway led directly into the clouds covering the high peak. Never had Hungry Heart seen a stairway stretch so long or so high before in her life! Unable to hide her disappointment, she sighed deeply. *It will take me days to climb these steps,* she thought.

With never a glance back in her direction, the assistant tied his boat securely to a mooring post. Satisfied with his knot, he motioned for Hungry Heart to follow him up the steps, rambling on about his busy life and how much he loved serving the Master. She had no opportunity at all to ask any questions! So she listened. According to him, he had the greatest appointment in all of Christianity: that of fetching travelers ready to approach the throne.

"No one ever believed that I would amount to anything. If they could see me now! But it doesn't matter that they can't see me, because what others think is not important anymore. What the Master thinks is the only thing that is important. No sirree, it is hard even for me to believe sometimes..."

Amazingly, they stepped into the dense misty cloud at the top in a matter of minutes. "Isn't this something!" the round little assistant marveled gleefully. "It's the Master's glory cloud! I've been up here hundreds of times, maybe even thousands, but I still get goose bumps when it touches me. Careful now, hold my hand if you get a little woozy. That happens sometimes, you know. Why, I've had people fall flat on their face right here before they even reach the doors. If that happens, it slows me down, yes sirree. If that happens, I'll have to sit right here, and wait for you to get up. Messes up my schedule, it does, but those are the orders from the Master."

Then, almost as an afterthought, he gave her hand a little tug and inquired, "How about it? Are your legs still underneath you there, lady? Not getting the glory shakes, are you?"

Her legs did feel a little uncertain, but Hungry Heart did not want to stop to rest. Unable to speak, she answered him by squeezing his hand and giving him a slight nod.

"Good for you! Just keep walking, and we'll be there before you know it," he encouraged her. "And by the way, don't worry about it if you can't say much. It's the way it's supposed to be. The Master does all the talking here, except for me, of course. I have special dispensations for my assignment. Someone has to help folks like you find their way in here or you'd all be piled up in a heap out there under the glory cloud. What a mess that'd be, wouldn't it now? I'd be trippin' over bodies all day long...that's a girl, just keep a'walkin' for me."

Eventually the sound of the assistant's voice grew softer and softer until Hungry Heart could not hear anything coming from his still-moving lips. Instead, soft musical tones drew her attention ahead. She thought she could see tiny golden sparkles floating through the cloud as they approached the enormous golden doors guarded by two very tall and very strong-looking assistants. The doors swung open at their announcement: "Hungry Heart is here at the Master's request."

Slowly Hungry Heart stepped through the open door into a grand circular room with a crystal clear glass floor. It mirrored every detail of the room, including the sparkle of seven enormous golden lamp stands and the Master's high majestic throne. There, on a throne that glowed like a golden red flame, sat the Master in unspeakable grandeur and awe, with a golden crown on his head. White-robed assistants and other travelers were already on their faces before him, and Hungry Heart fell to her knees speechless. For the first time in her life, even her heart stood silent.

Then, as if she was the only one in his presence, he spoke directly to her in a heart-to-heart conversation. His lips did not move, nor did hers. Their hearts united in perfect harmony and understanding. Constrained by the gentle yet growing weight of the glory cloud, she lowered the rest of her body and lay face down on the floor motionless. Her body, mind, and heart submitted to waves of sublime peace. Here, before his magnificent throne, she sensed his complete acceptance and gave herself completely to his service. She allowed his words free access to every corner of her mind.

"Hungry Heart, there are three things that I have brought you here for. First, I give you a new name. You have died to the hunger that once consumed you, and in dying you now have a new heart, one of compassion and tenderness. From this time forward, you shall be known by all as 'Tender Heart.'

"Second, I designate your appointment. I am sending you back to the kingdom of Christianity to tell as many people as you possibly can about my dwelling place, to tell them that it is here waiting for them when they are ready. But tell them only what they need to know to begin their journey—nothing more and nothing less. Speak into their hearts and point them to me. I will teach them on the way as I have done for you.

"Finally, your paradigm quest is complete. After you relinquished your paradigm pieces and entered the third gateway, they were sent here to me. I have created this paradigm to help you tell others about my dwelling place. It is complete, just as my love for you is complete."

His strong hands reached out and touched her trembling shoulders. "Rise, Tender Heart, and receive your paradigm."

Two assistants came forward and helped her rise from the floor to a kneeling position, that she might accept her completed paradigm from the Master. Weakened by the sheer wonder of his glorious appearance, her hands quivered so badly that one of the assistants reached out to steady them for her. As soon as the assistant touched her hands, the shaking stopped. The other assistant placed his hand on her head, and strength poured back into her body, beginning at her head and neck and continuing down through her torso and limbs. Then, as quietly as they appeared, they stepped back and disappeared, leaving her completely alone with the Master.

Suspended in time itself, he allowed her to treasure every precious moment of this encounter. His eyes gave her permission to simply rest in his total and complete love without any pressure to be or do anything other than to bask in the all-consuming "now" moment, which stretched back to the beginning of time and forward into eternity. She did not comprehend it, nor did she attempt to. The experience completely transcended her own finite existence and plunged her into the unspeakable mysteries of her Master's kingdom someplace between the heavens and the earth.

Compelled to protect her from transcending earth completely, the Master's all-knowing love reached out and drew her safely back to the shores of substance by placing the completed paradigm in her hands. Like waking up from a beautiful dream, her eyes focused on the magnificently crafted piece in her hands.

Beginning at the bottom, seven intricate gold and silver engravings mapped the Great Refinery, the Lagoon of Truth, the Village of Enlightenment, the City of Bread, the Gardens of Devotion, the Golden Throne Room, and his throne. Every paradigm piece she had received since childhood, complete with the precious gemstones, formed a perfect picture of the Master's Dwelling Place.

Tender Heart ran her hands lovingly over every detail, almost unable to believe that this priceless treasure belonged to her. Yet here it was in her hands, marking her personal journey with the Master since childhood. Every piece fit together perfectly. Her paradigm quest was complete. Tears slipped from her eyes in unbridled love and appreciation for the Master as she realized her victory's bittersweet sorrow. This meant the end. Unable to look into his eyes, her quivering lips whispered, "Master, have I come so far only to return home? You said that you were going to take me so far that I would never be able to go back. I thought that I would be staying here with you on one of your mountains."

"Tender Heart, remember, it matters not how far you have come, but why you have come, doesn't it?" Humbled with his wisdom and confronted with the simple truth that had followed her over every mountain, she nodded in silent agreement while he continued.

"I am not sending Hungry Heart back. Hungry Heart will never be able to go back. Instead, I am sending you, Tender Heart. The choice, as always, is yours. You may spend the rest of your life here, at the foot of my throne. However, your heart is tender now, and it will hear others calling out for compassion.

"You know the way in and the way out. You are free to embark on journeys anywhere on these mountains for as often and as long as you desire. In fact, there will be times when I will call you to come aside with me for a special purpose. This is not the last time your feet will walk these mountains. No, you will travel from one end to the other many times over. You will continue to learn and grow and walk with me in new ways. You see, your paradigm has all the necessary elements to tell the story, but your life understanding is far from completion.

"Your heart longed for your completed paradigm and your appointment. Now they are yours. What you do with your paradigm will be up to you. You may keep it close to your heart and continue to enjoy many won-derful moments together with me. Or you may openly share it with those whom I will place in your pathway, just as others have done for you. The choice is yours. You now have your life-message, but your life will find completeness only as you go where this message takes you."

"How will I find my way home?" Tender Heart asked quietly, raising her eyes to his.

The Master stepped back slightly, to depart with this word: "Your tender heart knows the way. Follow it. Besides, you aren't going alone. I am with you always."

Clutching the paradigm between her hands, Tender Heart bowed rever-ently and carefully stepped back between other travelers still on their knees before the Master. At the golden doors, she hesitated and looked back. Her heart ached painfully because she did not want to leave the glory of this place. Her tear-filled eyes pleaded with the assistant who stood beside her, ready to lead her out. Could she have more time? He quietly acknowledged her request and moved aside.

Tender Heart found a quiet place of solitude and lingered underneath the glory cloud, watching the golden flecks fall over and around her like sparkling raindrops. Closing her eyes, she tried very hard to remember every detail of this throne room. She wanted to stay as long as possible, but her thoughts of home grew stronger and stronger until it became difficult to concentrate. From time to time, she heard voices calling for her to come and help them. As much as she loved the Master's throne, her heart yearned to serve him.

A few moments later she nodded to the assistant and followed him out through the golden doors, down the mountain staircase, and to the little boat where the short, round-faced assistant stood waiting for her with more questions that she could possibly answer.

"All finished up there, little lady? Wasn't it grand? Did you fall down under the glory cloud? Most folks do! I see you have a new name, and a fine one it is, too. I'll bet you can't wait to get home to tell everyone about your adventures, can you? Well, let's get started. The Master asked me to take you back over the lake and down the river to the Second Mountain. How about one more boat ride, now that you have your sea legs again?"

Tender Heart took one last look over her shoulder as the shoreline dis-appeared from view. Wisely, the assistant knew that it was still quite impossible for her to speak, so he kept talking and recounted his different adventures to her all the way back to the Second Mountain. Tender Heart simply smiled and nodded at the appropriate times.

As they docked at the foot of the Second Mountain, not far from the Gardens of Devotion, the assistant said good-bye with one last thought. "Come back soon, Tender Heart, and bring someone with you next time!"

Tender Heart's journey back over the mountains to the Plains of Hope was pleasant and quite uneventful in comparison to her adventures on the way in. She passed travelers on the way, visited with friends, and took plenty of time to study the Great Book. Her steps were lighter and the distance between cities seemed remarkably shorter this time. There were fewer distractions and less temptations to leave the main road, though the spirit creatures still made noise and relentless hearts occasionally badgered her to stay in this place or that place. After all, the paradigm hanging from a golden chain around her neck did draw attention. Curious hearts often followed her for short times, but she kept moving westward.

Every time Tender Heart studied the paradigm, now hanging on a golden chain around her neck, she discovered something new. One time she found the miniature castle piece embedded in the delicate engraving of the Master's throne room. This miniature castle piece depicted the throne room in her own heart. So in one sense, her journey had taken her into the very center of her own heart.

True to his word, the Master always remained close at hand. Sometimes they looked like two travelers walking side by side and at other times she appeared quite alone, conversing with him heart to heart. More often than not, she contentedly watched him with other travelers. On her way in she had been preoccupied with her own journey and rarely, if ever, in fact, saw the Master helping anyone else.

Now her tender heart watched him help traveler after traveler, just as he had done for her. He encouraged everyone who looked his way and never admonished the ones who rushed by him or strayed from the main roadway. Tender Heart watched, and listened, and learned about his abounding tender love.

When the Master and Tender Heart reached the Gardens of Devotion, they paused for a short time outside the Garden of Refining Fire. Tender Heart closed her eyes and remembered how the Master's fire came to her when she did not have the strength or the ability to reach it herself. She still failed to understand what had happened to her in those moments or why she had not been totally destroyed in the hungry flames.

"Master, will I ever understand?" she asked.

"Someday you will able to see your experience from a great distance, and then you will understand. Right now you are too close to see the beginning from the end. Patience, Tender Heart. If you will always be as patient with yourself as you are with others, your journey will be much easier."

In the City of Bread they supped at the golden table and stopped by to visit with the bread vendors. Much to her surprise, the Master accepted gifts of bread from the vendors, and he suggested that she do the same.

"Now that your heart is tender, you can perceive the sincerity in their hearts. Their bread will never satisfy you in the same way that the bread of my bounty does, but the compassion in your heart will reach out to accept their gifts regardless of the reward."

Searching Heart met them at the edge of the Village of Enlightenment and accompanied them to the closest lamp stand where Tender Heart told her paradigm story beneath the soft rainbow of lamplight. Travelers sitting under the light leaned forward to catch every word, asking questions for hours until Tender Heart managed to convince them to seek the Master themselves for the answers.

She found Sacrificial Heart at the Lagoon of Truth and waited patiently for her to finish helping a new traveler from the Great Refinery wash in the waters of truth. Afterwards they walked together back past the Great Refinery and watched the dancing flames. Tender Heart remembered the heartbreaking task of feeding the Master's fire until she discovered the dead wood in her own life that satisfied its hunger.

"It seems like only yesterday...I wonder how long I have been gone?" Tender Heart mused thoughtfully.

Sacrificial Heart waited for the Master's nod of approval, then answered Tender Heart's question, bringing her journey full circle.

"In terms of your life, Tender Heart, you have been traveling for a very long time, almost an entire lifetime. As for your family and friends back on the Plains of Hope, do not be surprised if they haven't even noticed your absence. You were never more than a hopeful thought away from them at any time.

"Remember the assistant's words when you entered the first gateway? Day and night do not measure time in the Master's dwelling place. It is only measured by the changes that take place in your heart. It is not how far you have traveled that mattered, but why you have traveled. The majority of people are not going to be impressed by the length of your journey or even by your magnificent paradigm. The only thing the Master wants them to see is your tender heart—and see it they will. Come now, I'll go back through the catacombs with you."

They entered the catacombs and passed large groups of travelers coming in from the first gateway. Just as Sacrificial Heart foretold, no one appeared to notice Tender Heart or the beautiful paradigm hanging around her neck. They were all preoccupied with their own journeys and trying to decide whether or not to carry their bags and satchels, just as she once had. The two friends parted at the gateway where Sacrificial Heart gave her a big hug and laughed, "I think you know your way home from here."

Back home, on the Plains of Hope, life looked pretty much the same. Most of the damage caused by the North Wind was still under repair, and people moved about their daily lives under the Master's watchful eye. She passed several meeting places on the way, and they, too, were still in the midst of renovations. By the time she reached Grandfather Humble Heart's street, she could she that Mr. Able Heart's lawn was being replanted and Elder Stubborn Heart's house was going to be rebuilt.

After checking Grandfather Humble Heart's house and finding a note to say that he and her parents were still down in the Valley of Despair taking care of broken and disappointed hearts, she walked through the village, waving and greeting old friends. Some people recognized her from a distance and called out, "Tender Heart, you have a new name! How wonderful! Welcome home!" Others simply acknowledged her new name and sent their greetings as if she had never left.

Beyond the laughter, the busy street noise and the sounds of children playing, Tender Heart heard a faint cry coming from one of the meeting places. It drew her like a magnet, and she stepped inside to find a young rebellious heart weeping over a copy of the Great Book. It was a strange sight indeed. Rebellious hearts were not known for their devotion to the Great Book or for their appreciation for the meeting places. No, they were usually found on the outskirts of town where no one cared about their unruly behavior and unorthodox manner of dress.

"Rebellious Heart, is there anything I can do?" Tender Heart asked softly.

The rebellious heart did not even look up. He just stared at the Great Book in his hands and wept, "There's too much here. I can't possibly learn it all, yet the elder religious hearts in my family expect me to read, study, and understand all of this...and what for? There are already too many people here who know too much and too few who care. Why should I join the endless parade of religious hearts who continually march in circles without going anywhere?"

"What does your heart want to do?"

Stunned that anyone cared enough to ask, he looked right past Tender Heart and stared out the door toward the mountains.

"My heart wants to fly to the top—no, even beyond those mountains— and sing songs of joy about the Master for the rest of my life. Yet, because I cannot follow in the footsteps of my elder religious hearts, my heart has turned rebellious and I am an outcast."

"You want to go to the Mountains of Joy?" she asked.

"No, I've been to the Mountains of Joy...it's good, but it's not enough. I want more! I want to go...I'm not certain where I want to go, except that I do not want to stay here any longer..."

With that his eyes focused on Tender Heart, then locked on the beautiful paradigm hanging from around her neck. Speechless, he looked and then looked again. He grabbed the Great Book and started flipping the pages as fast as he could.

"Here, here it is...the story of the Master's dwelling place where one finds the desires of his heart. You have been there; you have been beyond the Mountains of Joy...I cannot live like this any longer! I must learn to fly with the eagles on the mountains and sing with birds in the heavens! I must have more, or I will die!"

"Let him finish," the Master whispered to her heart. "No one else will listen to him."

Tender Heart waited patiently and allowed him to pour out his heart as honestly as he knew how. To his religious elders, his words would have been considered quite rebellious, but Tender Heart heard something else. She waited patiently for him to ask the question that needed to be asked. After he emptied all the rebellion from his heart, he reached out to touch her paradigm, lowered his eyes and whispered meekly, "Please, tell me the story."